MOSCOW

TO THE END OF THE LINE

EUROPEAN CLASSICS

Honoré de Balzac	*The Bureaucrats*
Heinrich Böll	*And Never Said a Word* *And Where Were You, Adam?* *The Bread of Those Early Years* *End of a Mission* *Irish Journal* *Missing Persons and Other Essays* *A Soldier's Legacy* *The Train Was on Time*
Madeleine Bourdouxhe	*La Femme de Gilles*
Lydia Chukovskaya	*Sofia Petrovna*
Aleksandr Druzhinin	*Polinka Saks • The Story of Aleksei Dmitrich*
Venedikt Erofeev	*Moscow to the End of the Line*
Konstantin Fedin	*Cities and Years*
Fyodor Vasilievich Gladkov	*Cement*
I. Grekova	*The Ship of Widows*
Marek Hlasko	*The Eighth Day of the Week*
Erich Kästner	*Fabian: The Story of a Moralist*
Ignacy Krasicki	*The Adventures of Mr. Nicholas Wisdom*
Karin Michaëlis	*The Dangerous Age*
Andrey Platonov	*The Foundation Pit*
Arthur Schnitzler	*The Road to the Open*
Ludvík Vaculík	*The Axe*

MOSCOW
TO THE END OF THE LINE

Venedikt Erofeev

Translated by H. William Tjalsma

NORTHWESTERN UNIVERSITY PRESS
Evanston, Illinois

Northwestern University Press
www.nupress.northwestern.edu

Printed in the United States of America

15 14 13 12 11 10 9

ISBN-13: 978-0-8101-1200-1
ISBN-10: 0-8101-1200-0

Library of Congress Cataloging-in-Publication Data

Erofeev, Venedikt, 1933–
   [Moskva-Petushki. English]
   Moscow to the end of the line / Venedikt Erofeev ; translated by
H. William Tjalsma.
     p. cm. — (European classics)
   ISBN 0-8101-1200-0 (alk. paper)
   I. Tjalsma, H. William. II. Title. III. Series: European
classics (Evanston, Ill.)
   [PG3479.7.R59M613   1994]
   891.73'44—dc20   94–20616
                                               CIP

To Vadim Tikhonov,

my beloved firstborn,

I dedicate these tragic

pages.

MOSCOW

TO THE END OF THE LINE

The first edition of *Moscow to the End of the Line* was sold out quickly, thanks to its being an edition of one copy. I have often been chastised since then for the chapter "Hammer & Sickle—Karacharovo," quite without reason. In the Introduction to the first edition, I warned all the girls that they ought to skip the chapter "Hammer & Sickle—Karacharovo," since, after the phrase "And I drank it straight down," there followed nothing but pure obscenity—since, in the entire chapter, save for the phrase "And I drank it straight down," there was not a single printable word. With this conscientious advice I only assured that all readers—in particular the girls—would head right for the chapter "Hammer & Sickle—Karacharovo," without even reading the previous chapters, without even so much as reading the words "And I drank it straight down." For this reason, I have considered it necessary in this second edition to toss out of the chapter "Hammer & Sickle—Karacharovo" all the indecent words. It'll be better that way, because, for one thing, people will read me from the beginning through and, for another, no one will be offended.

—*V. E.*

Everyone says, "The Kremlin, the Kremlin." I hear about it from everybody, but I've never seen it myself. How many times (thousands) I've walked, drunk or hung over, across Moscow from north to south, east to west, from one end to the other, one way or another, and never did I see the Kremlin.

Take yesterday. Again I didn't see it, and I spent the whole evening wandering around those parts, and I wasn't even so drunk. As soon as I came out of the Savelovo Station I had a glass of Zubrovka to start with, since I know from experience that they've not come up with anything better by way of an eye-opener.

So. A glass of Zubrovka. Then later, on Kaliaevsky Street, another, only not Zubrovka this time but Coriander. One of my acquaintances says that Coriander vodka has an antihuman effect on a person; that is, it strengthens all the physical members but weakens the soul. With me it happened the other way around for some reason; that is, my soul was strengthened in the highest degree while my members were weakened. But I agree that this too is antihuman. Therefore, at the same time, I added two mugs of Zhiguli beer and an Albe de dessert port straight from the bottle.

Of course you'll ask, "Then what, Venichka, then what did you drink?" But I can't figure out what I drank next. I remember—this I remember clearly—on Chekhov Street I downed two glasses of Hunter's. But really, could I cut across the Sadovy Circle without a drink? No, I couldn't. Which means I drank something else.

Then I headed for the center of town, since it always works out that when I'm looking for the Kremlin I end up at the Kursk Station. In fact, I really did have to go to the Kursk Station and not the center of town, but I set out for the center all the same in order to see the Kremlin at least once, meanwhile thinking, "I won't see any Kremlin anyway and I'll end up right at the Kursk Station."

Now I'm almost in tears feeling sorry for myself. Not because I didn't get to the Kursk Station yesterday, of course. (That's nonsense—if not yesterday, then today I'll get there.) Naturally not because I woke up this morning in some unfamiliar front hallway or other. (It turns out that I sat down on a step in the hallway, the fortieth from the bottom by count, grasped my suitcase to my heart, and fell asleep like that.) No, I'm not feeling sorry because of that. No, I'm sorry because I just calculated that from Chekhov Street to this hallway I drank up six rubles—but where and what and in what sequence, to good or evil purpose? This nobody knows and, now, nobody will ever know. Just as we don't know to this day whether Tsar Boris killed the Tsarevich Dmitri or the other way around.

What sort of a hallway was it? I haven't the slightest idea even now, and it ought to be that way. Everything should. Everything should take place slowly and incorrectly so that man doesn't get a chance to start feeling proud, so that man is sad and perplexed.

I came outside when it was already getting light. Everyone knows—everyone who has ended up out cold in a hallway and left at dawn—everyone knows what a heavy heart I carried down those forty steps in a strange hallway, and what a weight I carried outside.

"It's nothing," I said to myself. "Nothing. There's a pharmacy, see? And over there, that creep in the brown jacket scraping the sidewalk. You see that too? So calm down. Everything is going along as it should. If you want to turn left, Venichka, turn left, I'm not forcing you to do anything. If you want to turn right, turn right."

I turned right, staggering a bit from the cold and from grief, yes, from the cold and from grief. Oh, that morning burden in the heart! Oh, the illusory nature of calamity. Oh, the irretrievable! What's worse about this burden which no one has yet called by any name, what's worse—paralysis, or nausea? Nervous exhaustion, or mortal sorrow somewhere in the region of the heart? But, if that's all equal, then all the same what's worse about it—stupefaction, or fever?

"It's OK, it's OK," I said to myself. "Back to the wind and get going slowly. And breathe slow, slow. Breathe so that your knees don't get tangled. Go on, anywhere. It's all the same where. Even if you turn left, you'll end up at the Kursk Station; or straight, all the same, the Kursk Station. Therefore, turn right, so that you'll get there for sure. Oh, vanity.

"Oh, the ephemeral! Oh, that most helpless and shameful of times in the life of my people, the time from dawn until the liquor stores open up! How many unnecessary gray hairs has it caused us homeless and grieving brunets! Let's go, Venichka, let's go."

There you are. I *did* know what I was talking about. You turn right and inevitably you get to the Kursk Station. You were bored there in the back alleys, Venichka, and you wanted to rub elbows with the crowd, so there you are.

"Oh, forget it." I gave myself the brush-off. "Do I really need your crowd? Are your people really necessary? Take the Redeemer even, who to his own Mother said, "What art thou to me?" And, indeed, what do these vain and repellent creatures have to do with me?

"I'd better lean up against a column and screw up my eyes, so I won't feel so sick."

Of course, Venichka, of course, someone sang out on high, so softly, so tenderly, tenderly. *Screw up your eyes so you won't feel so sick.*

Oh! I recognize them. It's them again! The angels of God! It's you again.

But of course it's us. Again, so tender!

"You know, angels?" I asked, also softly, softly.

What? the angels answered.

"It's tough for me."

Yes, we know that it's tough, the angels sang out. *But get moving, you'll feel better, and the stores will be open in half an hour—no vodka until nine, it's true, but they'll have a little red the first thing.*

"Red wine?"

A little red wine, the angels of God chorused.

"Chilled?"

Chilled, of course.

Oh, I got terribly excited.

16

"You say get moving, you'll feel better. But I don't feel like moving at all. You know yourselves what sort of shape I'm in . . . to get moving!"

The angels kept quiet about that. And then started singing again.

You know what, drop by the restaurant at the Station. They've got something there. Yesterday, they had sherry. It couldn't have been all drunk up in one evening.

"Yes, yes, yes. I'll go. I'll go right now and find out. Thank you, angels."

Your health, Venya.

And then ever so gently:

Don't mention it.

They're so nice. . . . Well, let's . . . get moving then . . . It's a good thing I bought some goodies yesterday—you can't go to Petushki without goodies. It was the angels who reminded me about the goodies, because I bought them for the ones who are themselves like angels. It's a good thing you bought them. When, yesterday, did you buy them? Remember . . . Walk and try to remember. . . .

I walked across the square. Rather, I was drawn across it. I stopped two or three times and froze on the spot in order to get the queasiness under control. Because, after all, a person has more than just a physical side. He has a spiritual side as well and, more than that, there's a mystical, a superspiritual side. So, there I was in the square expecting any minute to get sick on all three sides. And, again, I'd stop and freeze.

"So, when was it you bought your goodies yesterday? After the Hunter's? No, after the Hunter's I wasn't up to buying presents. Between the first and second glass of Hunter's? No, between the two glasses there was a break of thirty seconds, and I'm not superhuman and able to get something done in thirty seconds. Anyway, a superhuman being would have collapsed after the first glass of Hunter's and never made it to the second. So when was it? By the grace of God, how many mysteries there are in the world! An impenetrable veil of mysteries. Before the Coriander or between the beer and the Albe de dessert?''

MOSCOW. THE KURSK STATION RESTAURANT

"No, not between the beer and the Albe de dessert for sure. There was no break then at all. So, probably before the Coriander, that's quite possible. Or, more likely, I bought the nuts before the Coriander but the candy after. Or, perhaps, the other way around. When I'd drunk the Coriander, I . . .''

"There's nothing to drink,'' the bouncer said. And he looked me over as if I were a little dead bird or a filthy buttercup. "No, nothing alcoholic.''

Though I cringed in desperation, all the same I managed to mumble that I hadn't come for that anyway. It's none of his damned business why I was there. Perhaps the Perm Express didn't want to go to Perm for some reason and so I came to eat beef Stroganoff and listen to Ivan Kozlovsky or something from *The Barber of Seville*.

I had taken my little suitcase with me anyway, and, just as back there in the front hallway, I squeezed it to my heart, expecting a command.

Nothing to drink! Mother of God! Indeed, if you believe

the angels, they're fairly drowning in sherry in here. But now there's only music and music with some kind of mangy harmonics at that. Yes, that's Ivan Kozlovsky all right. I recognized him immediately; there's no one else with a voice that nauseous. All singers have equally nauseous voices, but every one of them is nauseous in its own way. That's why I can identify them so easily. Well, of course: Ivan Kozlovsky. "Oh, Chalice of my fore-bear-ers, Oh, let me gaze for-e-ever upon you by star-r-r-r light." Well, of course: Ivan Kozlovsky. "Oh, why am I smi-i-tten so with you. Don't reje-e-ect me."

"Will you be ordering anything?"

"What've you got, just music?"

"What do you mean, just music? Beef Stroganoff, pastries, udder . . ."

I felt sick again.

"What about sherry?"

"No sherry."

"Interesting, you serve udder but not sherry."

"Verrry interesting. Right, no sherry, but udder we've got."

And I was left alone. So as not to get sicker I started to examine the chandelier above my head.

It was a good chandelier. But really too heavy. If it should break away and fall on someone's head, it'd be terribly painful. Well, no, probably not even painful. While it's tearing away and falling, you're sitting, not suspecting a thing—drinking sherry, for instance. But as soon as it hits you, you're dead. A weighty thought, that . . . you're sitting there and a chandelier falls from above. A very weighty thought. But, really, why so weighty? If, let's say, you've been drinking sherry, if you're good and drunk and haven't yet succeeded in getting hung over, and they don't give you any sherry, and then you get a chandelier in the head, that's weighty. A very oppressive thought. One not everyone has the strength to endure, especially when dead drunk.

And you'd agree to it, if they'd bring you, let's say, 800 grams of sherry in return for which they'd unhook the chandelier over your head and . . .

"So, have you made up your mind? Are you ordering something or not?"

"Eight-hundred grams of sherry, please."

"You're already doing well enough, obviously. You were told in plain Russian we don't have any sherry."

"So . . . I'll wait . . . until you've got it . . ."

"Wait, wait . . . You'll get your sherry all right."

Again, I'm left alone. As she left, I looked at the woman with repulsion. Especially at her white stockings without any seams—a seam would have made me feel at peace, perhaps even unburdened my soul and my conscience.

Why are they all so crude? Eh? And so blatantly crude at the very moment when one oughtn't to be crude, when a person has all his nerves dangling out, when he is chicked-hearted and placid? Why is it always like that? Oh, if only the whole world, if everyone were like I am now, placid and timorous and never sure about anything, not sure of himself nor of the seriousness of his position under the heavens—oh, how good it could be. No enthusiasts, no feats of valor, nothing obsessive! Just universal chicken-heartedness. I'd agree to live on the earth for an eternity if they'd show me first a corner where there's not always room for valor. "Universal chicken-heartedness." Indeed this is the panacea, this is the predicate to sublime perfection. And as for nature's activist inclinations . . .

"Who's getting sherry here?"

Looming above me were two women and a man, all three in white. I looked up at them and, oh, how much ugliness and vagary there must have been in my eyes then. I knew that just by looking at them, because my ugliness and vagary were reflected in their eyes. I felt myself sinking somehow and losing a hold on my soul.

"Yes, well, I'm . . . almost not asking. Well, so, there isn't any sherry, I'll wait, I'll just . . ."

"Whadaya mean 'just'? What do you think you're going to 'wait' for?"

"Oh, nothing much. I'm just going to Petushki, to a beloved young lady." To a beloved young lady, ha, ha. "I've bought some goodies, see."

They waited, the executioners, to see what I would say next.

"I'm . . . from Siberia, I'm just a kid. And just so I won't get sick, I'd like some sherry."

Pointlessly, I mentioned sherry again and that set them off at once. All three of them grabbed me under the arms and led me—oh, the pain of such a disgrace—across the entire Station and shoved me outside. And, after me, my little suitcase with the goodies.

Outside again. Oh, emptiness, oh, the bared fangs of existence.

What it was like from the restaurant to the store and from the store to the train, human language cannot bend itself to describe. I won't try either. And if the angels should take it up, they'll break into tears and the tears will prevent them from getting anywhere.

Instead, let's do this: let's honor those two deadly hours with a minute of silence. Remember those two hours, Venichka. In the most ecstatic, in the most sparkling days of your life, remember them. In moments of bliss and rapture, do not forget them. They should not be repeated. I turn to all who are kindred, to all people of good will, I turn to all whose hearts are open to poetry and fellow feelings:

"Leave what you're doing. Stop together with me and honor with a minute of silence that which is inexpressible. If you've got any kind of an old noisemaker, whistle, or horn handy, let's hear it."

So. I also stop. Exactly one minute, standing like a column in the middle of the Kursk Station Square, I stare darkly at the Station clock. My hair one moment flying in the wind, now standing on end, now flying again with taxis flowing around me on all four sides. People, too, and they look at me wildly, undoubtedly thinking, "Should he be sculpted like that for the edification of the people of the future, or not?"

And the silence is broken only by a husky female voice pouring down from nowhere.

"Attention. Leaving from siding number four at 8:16,

the train for Petushki. Stops in Hammer & Sickle, Chukhlinka, Reutovo, Zheleznodorozhnaya, and beyond at all stations except Esino."

But I remain standing.

"I repeat. Leaving from siding number four at 8:16, the train for Petushki. Stops in Hammer & Sickle, Chukhlinka, Reutovo, Zheleznodorozhnaya, and beyond at all stations except Esino."

Well, that's it. The minute has passed. Now, of course, everyone pounces on me with questions. "Hey, you get some booze, Venichka?"

"Yes, I tell you, I've got some." And I continue walking in the direction of the platform, inclining my head to the left.

"Your suitcase is heavy now, right? And there's a song in your heart, right?"

"The suitcase is heavy, that's right. But as far as my heart goes, it's too early to tell."

"All the same, Venichka, so what did you buy? We're *terribly* interested."

"Yes, I can tell. Just a minute, I'll list it all: first, two bottles of Kubanskaya for two sixty-two each; total, five twenty-four. Next, two quarter bottles of Rossiiskaya at a ruble sixty-four; total, five twenty-four plus three twenty-eight, eight rubles fifty-two kopeks. And then some red. Just a moment, I'll remember. Yes, stout rosé for one ruble thirty-seven."

"So-o-o," you say. "And the grand total? This is really terribly interesting."

"The grand total is nine rubles eighty-nine kopeks," I

say, stepping onto the platform. "But that's not really the grand total. I also bought a couple of sandwiches so as not to puke."

"You mean 'so as not to throw up,' Venichka?"

"No, what I said I said. I can't take the first dose without a bit to eat, because I might puke otherwise. But the second and third now, I can drink straight, because it's OK to feel sick, but I won't start puking no matter what. Right up to number nine. And, there, I need another sandwich."

"How come? You'll throw up again?"

"Oh, no, I won't throw up for anything. But as for puking, I'll puke."

Of course, you all nod your heads at that. I even see from here, from the wet platform, how all of you scattered about my world are nodding your heads and getting ready to be ironic.

"How complicated that is, Venichka, how subtle!"

"You said it."

"Such clarity of thought. And that's all it takes to make you happy? Nothing more?"

"What do you mean, 'nothing more?' " I say, getting on the train. "If I'd had more money I would have taken along some beer and a couple of bottles of port, but unfor—"

Here, you really begin to moan.

"O-o-o-o, Venichka! O-o-o, you primitive."

"So what of it? So I'm a 'primitive,' " I say. But I'm not going to answer any more of your questions. I'll just sit here hugging my suitcase to my heart and looking out the window. Like this. A "primitive." Fine!

While you go on pestering me.

"What's with you. Offended?"

"Course not," I answer.

"Don't get offended, we wish you well. Only why are you such a fool hugging your suitcase to your heart? Because the vodka is in there, is it?"

Now I'm thoroughly offended. What's the vodka got to do with it?

"Attention, passengers, this train goes to Petushki. Stops in Hammer & Sickle, Chukhlinka, Reutovo, Zheleznodorozhnaya, and beyond at all stations, except Esino."

After all, what's the vodka got to do with it? Aren't you sick of talking about the vodka? In the restaurant I was hugging it to my heart, and there was no vodka in it then. And in the hallway, if you remember, I also hugged it close, though there wasn't even a whiff of vodka in it yet. If you want to know everything, I'll tell you, but wait. I'll tie something on by Hammer & Sickle and

MOSCOW—HAMMER & SICKLE

then I'll tell everything, everything. Be patient. Aren't *I* being patient?

Well, of course, they all consider me a bad person. In the morning and hung over as I've been, I'm of the very same opinion about myself. But, after all, it's impossible to trust the opinion of a person who hasn't yet been able to tie one on. On the other hand, what chasms open up in me in the evening, if I've gotten good and looped during the day. What chasms.

But, so what. So what if I'm a bad person. I've noticed that, in general, if a person feels nasty in the morning but is full of plans and dreams and vigor in the evening, he's a very bad person. Mornings, rotten; evenings, fine—a sure sign of a bad type. But take someone who's full of energy and hope in the morning, but overwhelmed with exhaustion in the evening—for sure he's a trashy, narrow-minded mediocrity. That sort of person is disgusting to me. I don't know how he strikes you, but to me he's disgusting.

Of course, there are those for whom morning and evening are equally pleasing, who are equally pleased by sunrise and by sunset. These are simply bastards. It's sickening even to talk about them. But then, if someone is equally repulsed by morning and evening, I really don't know what to say about him. That's the ultimate cocksucking scum. Because our stores stay open till nine and you can always get something at the big Eliseev grocery up till eleven, so if you're not scum, by evening you'll always be able to create some sort of little chasm.

And so, what do I have here?

I took everything I had out of the suitcase and fingered it, from the sandwich to the stout rosé at a ruble thirty-seven. Touched it and suddenly started to grieve, and grew dim. . . . Lord, you see what I possess. But truly is *this* necessary to me? Truly is this what my soul is pained over? This is what people have given me in exchange for that over which my soul is pained. But if they had given me *that,* would I really be in need of *this?* Look, Lord, here's the stout rosé at a rub' thirty-seven.''

And, all in blue flashes of lightning, the Lord answered me:

"So what did St. Teresa need her stigmata for? It, too, was unnecessary, yet she desired it."

"That's the point," I answered in ecstasy. "Me, too, I desire this, but it's not at all necessary."

"Well, since it's desired, Venichka, go on and drink," I said to myself, but took my time. To see if perhaps the Lord had anything else to say.

The Lord was silent.

OK, then. I grabbed one of the quarter bottles and went out to the vestibule. Well, my spirit has grieved in confinement for four and a half hours—now I'll let it out to roam. I have a glass and a sandwich, so as not to throw up. And I have a soul, till now barely open to impressions of being. "Share with me my repast, Lord."

HAMMER & SICKLE—KARACHAROVO

And I drank it straight down.

KARACHAROVO—CHUKHLINKA

I drank it, and you saw how long I went on making a face and holding back the nausea, how I swore and cursed. Five minutes, seven minutes, a whole eternity I flung myself about like that, surrounded by four walls, grabbing myself by the throat, entreating God not to offend me.

Right up to Karacharovo, from Hammer & Sickle to Karacharovo, God was unable to hear my prayer. The glass I had drunk first seethed somewhere between the maw and the gullet, then billowed upward, then subsided again. It was like Vesuvius, Herculaneum, and Pompeii, like the First of May salute in my country's capital. And I suffered and prayed.

And it was only at Karacharovo that God heard my prayer and heeded it. Everything settled down and got quiet. And, with me, once anything gets quiet and settled down, it's irrevocable. Rest assured, I respect nature; it wouldn't be nice to return nature's gifts to her.

I smoothed my hair down a bit and returned to the car. The other passengers looked at me almost indifferently with their round, vacant eyes.

I like that. I like it that my country's people have such empty, bulging eyes. This instills in me a feeling of legitimate pride. You can imagine what the eyes are like where everything is bought and sold—deeply hidden, secretive, predatory and frightened. Devaluation, un-employment, pauperism . . . People look at you distrust-fully, with restless anxiety and torment. That's the kind of eyes they have in the world of Ready Cash.

On the other hand, my people have such eyes! They're constantly bulging but with no tension of any kind in them. There's complete lack of any sense but, then, what power! (What spiritual power!) These eyes will not sell out. They'll not sell or buy anything, whatever happens to my country. In days of doubt, in days of burdensome reflec-tion, at the time of any trial or calamity, these eyes will not blink. They don't give a good Goddamn about anything.

I like my people. I'm happy that I was born and grew up under the gaze of those eyes. There's only one thing bad about it, though. What if they noticed what I was up to in the vestibule—turning somersaults from one corner to the other, like the great Feodor Chaliapin in some tragedy, with my hand on my throat, as if something were choking me to death.

Any why not, let them. If anybody saw, all right. Perhaps I was rehearsing something out there? Right . . . come to think of it. Perhaps it was the immortal drama of *Othello, the Venetian Moor?* I was playing it alone—all the roles at once. I deceived myself, betrayed my convictions. Or else I had started to suspect myself of deceiving myself and betraying my convictions. I whispered in my ear about myself, oh, what I whispered! And there I am, in love with myself for my suffering—and I started to strangle myself. Grabbed myself by the throat to strangle myself. What's it to them what I was doing out there?

Look at that pair over there, on the right, next to the window. One of them is so stupid in his quilted jacket. But the other is so-o-o intelligent in his worsted overcoat. And, if you please, they're not embarrassed by anyone, pouring themselves drinks and putting it away. They don't run out to the end of the car wringing their hands. The stupid one drinks, grunts, and says, "Sonovabeech, not bad!" But the other, intelligent one drinks and says, "Tran-scen-den-tal!" And in such a festive voice. The stupid one takes a bite to eat and says, "Tastes fan-n-n-tastic today. Outa' this world." The so-o-o intelligent one chews and says, "Yes-s-s. Tran-scen-den-tal."

Incredible. I return to the car, wondering, had I been taken for a Moor, or did they think ill of me? While these two drink hearty in the open like the crown of existence, feeling superior to the whole world, I'm hung over in the morning and hide from heaven and earth, because this is the most intimate of intimacies. Before work, I drink on the sly. At work, I drink on the sly, but these two tran-scen-den-tal!

My delicate nature is indeed detrimental to me. It corrupted my childhood and adolescence. More precisely, it was not delicacy but simply that I had infinitely expanded the sphere of intimacy—how many times has this destroyed me.

I'll give you an example. I remember ten years ago I moved to Orokhovo-Zuevo. At that same time, there were four other people living in the same room. I was the fifth. We lived in complete harmony, and there weren't any quarrels among us. If someone wanted to drink port, he'd get up and say, "Boys, I want to drink port." And everyone would say, "Good, drink port. We'll drink port with you." If somebody was inclined to drink beer, everybody was inclined to drink beer.

Wonderful. But suddenly I started to notice that the four of them were somehow pushing me away. They would whisper amongst themselves, looking at me as I left the room. This was all a bit alarming for me. And I read the same preoccupation—fear, even—on their physiognomies. "What's the matter," I asked myself torturedly. "Why is this happening?"

And then came the evening when I understood what was what and why it was happening. As I recall that day, I never even got out of bed. I had drunk some beer and started grieving. So I simply lay there and grieved.

And all four of them quietly sat down around me, two on chairs at the head of the bed, and two at the foot, looking me reproachfully in the eye, with the bitterness of people unable to apprehend some secret locked within me. Just as if something had happened.

"Listen, you," they said. "Cut it out."

"Cut what out?" I said with surprise, sitting up.

"Cut out thinking that you're better than anyone else. That we're small potatoes and you're tops."

"Hey, what are you talking about?"

"This is what we're talking about. You drank beer today?"

CHUKHLINKA—KUSKOVO

"I did."

"A lot?"

"A lot."

"So get up and go."

"Go where?"

"As if you don't know. It works out like this: we're nothing but gnats and scoundrels and you're tops."

"Excuse me." I say, "I didn't suggest anything of the kind."

"You did suggest it. You suggested it every day since you moved in with us. Not in word but in deed. No, not even in deed, but by the absence of a deed. You negatively suggested it."

"What 'deed', what 'absence'?" I stared at them in wide-eyed amazement.

"You know what deed. You don't go to the toilet, that's what. We felt right away there was something funny. From the time you moved in we've not seen you go to the toilet once. OK, we're not speaking about number two. But not even number one, not even number one!"

All of this was said without a smile, in a deadly offended tone.

31

"No, boys, you don't understand me."

"We understand you perfectly."

"Wait, no, you don't. I simply can't get up from bed like you and announce publicly, 'Well, friends, I'm off to take a leak' or 'Well, boys, I'm going to take a crap.' I can't do that."

"And why can't you? We can, but you can't. It works out that you're better than we are. We're filthy animals and you're a lily."

"Not at all. . . . How can I explain it to you?"

"There's nothing to explain, it's all quite clear to us."

"Just listen . . . understand . . . in this world there are things . . ."

"We know as well as you do what kind of things there are and what there aren't. . . ."

I couldn't get anywhere with them. They had penetrated to my very soul with their morose expressions. I started to give in.

"Well, of course, I also can . . . I *could* . . ."

"That's it—you *can*, like us. But we *can't* like you. You can do anything, of course, while we are unable to do anything. You're tops and we're spit under your feet."

"No, no." Here I got completely muddled. "In this world there are spheres where it's impossible to simply get up and go. Because of self-restraint or whatever, the precepts of shame, from the days of Ivan Turgenev and, then, the idealism of Herzen's youth. And after that to get up and say, 'Well, boys. . . . It's insulting. I mean, supposing someone had a delicate heart . . ."

All four of them looked at me with mayhem in their eyes. I shrugged my shoulders and shut up, hopelessly.

"Forget about Ivan Turgenev. Be careful what you say. We've read him ourselves. You'd be better off saying whether you drank beer today."

"I did."

"How many bottles?"

"Two big ones and one small one."

"So get up and go. So we can all see you leave. Don't humiliate us and don't torture us. Get up and go."

So I got up and went. Not to relieve myself but to make things easier for them. And when I returned, one of them said to me, "With such feelings of shame you'll always be alone and unhappy."

Yes. He was absolutely right. I know many of God's intentions, but why he invested me with such chaste feelings I've never been able to figure out. And this chastity of mine—this is the funniest thing about it—this chastity of mine has been interpreted so inside out that I have been refused even the most elementary courtesies.

For instance, in Pavlovo-Posad. They take me to meet the ladies and present me like this:

"Here you have the very famous Venedikt Erofeev. He's well known for many reasons. But most of all, of course, for the fact that, in his whole life, he has never passed gas . . ."

"What! Never once?" The ladies are astonished and all eyes; they look me over. "Not once!"

I start getting flustered, of course. I cannot not get flustered in the presence of ladies. I say, "Well, not really, somehow! Sometimes . . . all the same . . ."

The ladies are even more astonished. "Erofeev! And . . . how strange . . . 'Sometimes, all the same'!"

I get completely flustered by all this and say something like, "Well . . . what's so, you know, I too . . . after all, it's—to pass gas—it's, after all, rather noumenal. There's nothing at all phenomenal about passing gas."

"Just think . . ." The ladies are crazy about all this.

But, later, they trumpet it all over the Petushki line that "he does it audibly, and he says that he does it not badly! That he does it quite well."

So, you see. And so it has been all my life. All my life this nightmare has haunted me, this nightmare of being understood not just wrongly, but in exactly the opposite way to what I intend.

I could tell you plenty about this subject, but if I start telling everything, I'll stretch it out as far as Petushki. I'd better give just one single case, because it's a completely fresh one—how, a week ago, they removed me from my post in the brigade for "introduction of a fallacious system of individualized charts." Our entire Moscow management quivers with fear whenever they merely remember those charts. And, really, what was so bad about them?

Where are we at the moment?

Kuskovo. We're going to barrel right through Kuskovo without stopping. I should have another drink on the occasion, but first I'd better tell you,

KUSKOVO—NOVOGIREEVO

and then I'll go out and have a drink.

So. A week ago I was kicked out of my job as brigade foreman, which I'd gotten five weeks ago. In four weeks, as you can understand, I couldn't have introduced any great changes, and even if anybody thought that I'd introduced any, all the same they didn't sack me for great changes.

Before I was made foreman, our work schedule looked like this: in the morning we'd sit down and play blackjack for money. Then we'd get up and unwind a drum of cable and put the cable underground. And then we'd sit down and everyone would take his leisure in his own way. Everyone, after all, has his own dream and temperament. One of us drank vermouth, somebody else—a simpler soul—some Freshen-up eau de cologne, and somebody else more pretentious would drink cognac at Sheremetievo International Field. Then we'd go to sleep.

First thing next morning, we'd sit around drinking vermouth. Then we'd get up and pull yesterday's cable out of the ground and throw it away, since, naturally, it had gotten all wet. And then what? Then we'd sit down to blackjack for money. And we'd go to sleep without finishing the game.

In the morning, we'd wake each other up early. "Lekha, get up. Time to play blackjack." "Stasik, get up and let's finish the game." We'd get up and finish the game. And then, before light, before sunrise, before drinking Freshen-up or vermouth, we'd grab a drum of cable and start to reel it out, so that by the next day it would get wet and become useless. And, so, then, each to each his own, for each has his own ideals. And so everything would start over again.

When I became foreman, I took this schedule to its logical conclusion. Now we did it this way: one day we'd play blackjack, the next we'd drink vermouth, on the third day, again blackjack, the fourth, vermouth again. And our intellectual, he disappeared altogether at Sheremetievo International—he just stayed there drinking cognac. We didn't so much as touch a cable drum, and if I'd even suggested touching one, the others would have started laughing like the gods, and then they would have beaten my face in with their fists, and then they would have gone their separate ways, playing blackjack for money, drinking vermouth, or drinking Freshen-up.

And until the end came, everything went splendidly. Once a month we'd send them our commemorative work projections and twice a month they'd send us our wages. We'd write, for instance, "On the occasion of the upcoming Lenin Centennial we undertake to eliminate work-related injuries." Or, we'd write, "On the occasion of the glorious Centennial we shall attain a part-time study rate in higher education of one out of every six workers." But what were work-related injuries and night school to us, if, because of blackjack, we didn't even get outside and there were altogether only five of us?

Oh, freedom and equality! Oh, brotherhood, oh, life on the dole! Oh, the sweetness of unaccountability, Oh, that most blessed of times in the life of my people, the time from the opening until the closing of the liquor stores.

Having discarded shame and cares for the future, we lived an exclusively spiritual life. I broadened their horizons as much as I was able, and they liked it when I did so, especially in matters concerning Israel and the Arabs. Here, they were in complete ecstasy, in ecstasy over Israel, in particular. And they couldn't stop talking about Golda Meir and King Farouk, whom I had mentioned by way of historical background. They would come in from whoring in the morning, and one of them, for instance, would say, "Goldie May-I" and another would answer, with a self-satisfied grin, "Farouk you!"

And later (listen carefully), later, after they had found out why Pushkin died, I gave them Alexander Blok's poem "The Nightingale Garden" to read. There, at the center of the poem—if you throw out all of the perfumed shoulders, the unilluminated mists, the rosy towers in smoky vestments—there at the center of the poem you find the lyric hero dismissed from work for drunkenness, whoring, and absenteeism. I told them, "It's a very contemporary book." I told them, "You'll find it useful." And so? They read it. But, in spite of everything, it had a depressing effect on them—Freshen-up disappeared immediately from all the stores. It's impossible to say why, but blackjack was forgotten, vermouth was forgotten, Sheremetievo International Field was forgotten, and Freshen-up triumphed. Everyone drank only Freshen-up. They drank up all the Freshen-up from Dolgoprudny Station to Sheremetievo International.

And then, suddenly, it dawned on me: "Venichka, what a blockhead you are, you're an out-and-out fool. Remember, you read in some man of wisdom that the Lord God only looks after the fate of princes, leaving the princes to look after the fate of the people. Well, you're the foreman and, therefore, a "little prince." Where is your concern for the fate of your people? Have you looked into the souls of those parasites, into their dark reaches? Are you familiar with the dialectic of the hearts of these four shitasses? You would do better to understand what 'The Nightingale Garden' and Freshen-up have in common and why 'The Nightingale Garden' is incompatible with both blackjack and vermouth, while Golda Meir and King Farouk are quite compatible with them.''

And so it was then I introduced my notorious individualized charts for which I was finally sacked.

Shall I tell you what kind of individualized charts they were? Now, that's simple: on white vellum in black India ink I drew two axes, one horizontal, the other vertical. All the workdays of the previous month were indicated sequentially on the horizontal axis, the amount of alcohol consumed—calculated on the basis of degree of proof—on the vertical axis. Of course, only whatever was consumed on the job or before was tabulated, since the amount consumed in the evening remained relatively constant, and was, therefore, of little interest to a serious researcher.

Thus at the end of the month the worker came to me with his report: on such and such a day, such and such an amount of such and such consumed, on another day so much of whatever. While I would illustrate all of that with a beautiful graph in black India ink on white vellum. Here, for you to admire, for instance, is the chart for Viktor Totoshkin, member of the Komosomol:

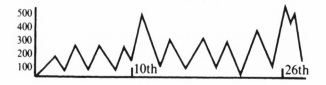

And this is Aleksei Blindiaev, member of the Communist Party of the Soviet Union since 1936, a seedy old dork:

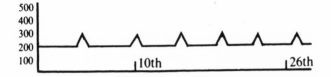

And here we have your faithful servant, ex-head cable-fitter and author of the poem *Moscow to the End of the Line:*

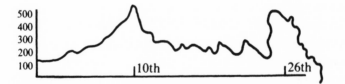

Aren't these truly interesting graphs? Interesting even to the most superficial eye? They looked variously like the Himalayas, the Tyrol, oil derricks, or even the Kremlin wall, which, admittedly, I have never seen.

Another one looked like a morning breeze on the Kama River, a gentle splash with rippling beads of lantern light. Still someone else's was like the beating of a proud heart, the song of the stormy petrel—in other words, pure

Gorky—or like Aivazovsky's trashy painting of the ninth wave. And all this, only looking at the external form of the line.

But, for anyone inquisitive (me, for instance), the lines blurted out everything that was possible to blurt out about the man and the heart of the man—all his qualities, from sexuality to practical matters as well as all his faults, both sexual and practical. Also, the degree of steadiness of temperament and of the tendency to treachery plus all his unconscious secrets, if he had any unconscious secrets.

I then examined with care, intently and close up, the soul of every shitass. But I didn't examine them for long—one fateful day all the charts disappeared from my desk. It seems that, on the same day, the old fogy Aleksei Blindiaev, member of the CPSU since 1936, sent off to the Administrative Section our obligatory holiday projection, in which we all swore, on the occasion of the upcoming Centennial, to be the same in our everyday life as at work. And, perhaps out of foolishness or perhaps drunkenness, he put my individualized charts into the same envelope.

As soon as I noticed them missing, I had a drink and grabbed my head. At the Administrative Section, also, they got the package, grabbed their heads, had drinks, and, the same day, drove into our district in their Moskvich. What did they uncover, bursting into our office? They uncovered nothing, except Lekha and Stasik—Lekha was dozing on the floor rolled up in a ball, and Stasik was puking. In a quarter of an hour everything was decided. My star, which had blazed forth for four weeks, passed from view. The crucifixion took place exactly thirty days after the ascension. There was but one month separating my Toulon from my Hélène. To put it bluntly, they canned me as foreman and in my place put that broken-down old dolt Aleksei Blindiaev, member CPSU, 1936. And, immediately after his designation, he got up from the floor and asked for a one-ruble note, which they did not give him. Stasik left off puking and also asked them for a rub', which they also didn't give him. They drank some red wine, got back in their Moskvich, and went back where they came from.

And so I solemnly announce that, till the end of my days, I shall not undertake anything the like of my sad brush with eminence. I'll remain below and from below I'll spit on their social ladder. Right, spit on every rung of it. In order to climb it, it's necessary to be forged steel-assed from head to toe. And this I'm not.

Anyway, they fired me. Me, the thoughtful prince, the analyst lovingly inspecting the souls of his people—me, who was considered, at the bottom, a fink and a collaborator and, at the top, a good-for-nothing with an unstable mind.

The lower strata did not wish to see me, and the higher-ups couldn't speak of me without laughing. "The top strata could not and the lower did not want to," as Lenin might have put it. What does this betoken, connoisseurs of the philosophy of history? Absolutely right—next payday, I'll get the shit beaten out of me, according to the laws of good and beauty, next payday being the day after tomorrow, which means that by the day after tomorrow they'll be kicking my ass around.

Whew!

"Who said 'Whew?' Is that you who said 'Whew,' angels?"

Yes, it was us. Whew, Venya, what language.

"So judge for yourselves, how could I help it? This whole mundane nonsense has gotten me so broken up that, since that very day, I haven't dried out. Before that I can't say I was especially dried out, but at least I used to remember what I drank and in what order. Now I can't even recollect that. Everything is ups and downs, everything in life is somehow up and down. First I don't drink for a week straight, then I drink for forty days, then again I don't drink for four days, and then I drink again for six months without a breather. Take now . . ."

We understand, we understand everything. They insulted you, you and your beautiful heart.

Yes, yes, on that day my beautiful heart struggled for a whole half hour with reason. As in the tragedies of the poet laureate Pierre Corneille, duty struggles with the heart's desire. But with me it was the reverse—the heart's desire struggled with reason and duty. The heart said to me, "They've insulted you, they've dragged you through shit. Go on and get drunk, Venichka, go on and get drunk as a skunk." This is what my beautiful heart said. But my reason? It grumbled and insisted, "You won't get up, Erofeev, you won't go anywhere and you won't drink a drop." While my heart responded, "Well, OK, Venichka, OK. You don't have to drink a lot. You don't have to get drunk as a skunk—drink 400 grams and let it go at that." "No grams at all," reason enunciated. "If you can't get along without anything, go on and drink three mugs of beer, Erofeev, and forget about the hard stuff." But my heart whimpered, "Maybe just 200 grams. Maybe . . .

42

. . . maybe just 150." And reason then: "Well, all right, Venya," it said, "all right, drink 150, only don't go out anywhere, stay home."

What do you think? Did I drink 150 and sit at home? Ha, ha. Since then I've drunk one and a half liters every day in order to sit home and all the same I don't sit home. Because on the sixth day I was so soused that the boundary between reason and heart had disappeared and they both recited in one voice: "Go, go to Petushki. In Petushki you'll find your salvation and your joy, go."

Petushki is the place where the birds never cease singing, not by day or by night, where winter and summer the jasmine never cease blooming. Perhaps there is such a thing as original sin, but no one ever feels burdened in Petushki. There, even those who don't dry out for weeks have a bottomless, clear look in their eyes.

There, every Friday, exactly at eleven o'clock, I'm met on the platform by that girl of the white eyes, white to off-white, that most beloved of trollops, that red-haired she-devil. And today is Friday. In less than two hours from now—exactly at eleven o'clock—she'll be there, with that whitish gaze in which there is no conscience and no shame. Come with me, oh, what things you will see. . . .

". . . And what did I leave behind, there, where I'm coming from? A pair of scraggly socks and work pants, pliers and a rasp, wages on account and overhead expenses—that's what I left behind. And what lies ahead? What waits on the platform in Petushki? Red lashes, downcast and heaving shapes and a braid from head to tail. And after the platform, Trapper's vodka and port wine, bliss and writhing, ecstasy and convulsions. Oh Heavenly Queen, how far is it to Petushki?

"And there beyond Petushki where the sky and the earth merge and the she-wolf howls at the stars, in a smoky, louse-infested mansion unknown to the whitish one, flowers the pudgiest and dearest of little ones—*my* little ones. He knows the letter *Ю* and expects some nuts from me for that. How many of you knew the letter *Ю* at three years? Not one. But he knows and doesn't expect any reward but a cupful of nuts.

"Pray for me, angels. Let my path be bright, let there be no stumbling block, let me see the city I have longed to see. And meanwhile—you forgive me—meanwhile look after my suitcase. I'm going away for ten minutes. I have to drink some Kubanskaya so that inspiration doesn't leave me."

And so I got up again and went down the car to the vestibule.

And I drank not as I did near Karacharovo, no, now I drank without nausea and without a sandwich, straight from the bottle, throwing back my head like a pianist, conscious both of the grandeur of the fact that it was just beginning and of what lay ahead.

NIKOLSKOE—SALTYKOVSKAYA

"These thirteen swallows will bring you no joy," I thought, taking the thirteenth.

"You know yourself that if you drink it from the bottle, the second morning dose beclouds the soul, even if it isn't for long—only up to the third dose taken from a glass—but all the same it beclouds the soul. Don't you know that?"

"So, let it. Let your future be bright. Let your tomorrow be even brighter. But why do the angels become troubled just as soon as you start talking about the joys of the Petushki platform and after?"

"Do they think that nobody is waiting for me there? Or that the train will be derailed, or that ticket inspectors will put me off in Kupavna? Or that somewhere around kilometer 105 I'll get sleepy from the wine and doze off and be strangled like a young boy or cut up like a little girl? Why are the angels troubled? Why have they fallen silent? My tomorrow is bright. Our tomorrow is brighter than our yesterday and our today. But who'll see to it that our day after tomorrow won't be worse than our day before yesterday?"

"Right, right. You put that well, Venichka. Our tomorrow and so on. That was nicely put and clever besides. But, in general, you don't have many brains. Don't you know yourself? Be at peace, Venichka, if only because your soul is roomier than your mind. What do you need a mind for, if you've got a conscience and, even more than that, taste? Conscience and taste—that's more than enough, making brains downright superfluous.

"When did you first notice that you're a fool, Venichka?"

"Here's when. When I was reproached at one and the same time for two things in polar opposition—for being both boring and frivolous. Because if someone is intelligent and boring he doesn't descend to frivolity. But if he is frivolous and intelligent, he won't permit himself to be

45

boring. Me, I'm a marshmallow who manages to be both.

"And should I tell why? Because I am sick in my soul, though I don't look it. Because, since that time, as I remember my condition, I do nothing but simulate mental health, expending everything, without a scrap left over, all powers, mental, physical, whatever. This is what makes me boring. Everything that you speak of, everything that occupies your time, is forever alien to me. While that which occupies me, I'll not say a word about. Maybe from fear I'll be taken for crazy, maybe from something else, but—all the same—not a word.

"I remember that, already a long time ago, when I would hear someone talking or arguing about some kind of nonsense, I would say, 'Eh, you really want to go into that nonsense?' And people would be amazed at that and say, 'In what way is this nonsense anyway? If this is nonsense, then what isn't?' And I'd say, 'Oh, I don't know, I don't know. But some things aren't.'

"I'm not saying that now the truth is known to me, or that I've approached it close up. Not at all. But I've gotten close enough to it so that it's convenient to look it over.

"And I look, and I see, and for that reason, I'm sorrowful. And I don't believe that any one of you has dragged around within himself this bitter, bitter mishmash. I'm in a quandary over saying what this mishmash is composed of, and, all the same, you would never understand, but mostly there's 'sorrow' and 'fear' in it. 'Sorrow' and 'fear' most of all and, then, muteness. And every day, the first thing in the morning, my 'beautiful heart' exudes this infusion and bathes in it till night. I know this happens with others if somebody dies suddenly, if the most important being on earth dies suddenly. But with me this is an eternal condition. At least understand this.

"How am I not to be boring and how am I not to drink Kubanskaya? I've earned the right. I know better than you that 'world sorrow' is not a fiction perpetrated by the old writers, because I carry it within myself and know what it is and I do not wish to hide this fact. One must get used to speaking of one's virtues bravely, to people's faces. Who is to know, if not we ourselves, to what degree we are good?

"For instance, do you know Kramskoy's painting, *Inconsolable Grief?* Well, of course you've seen it. Imagine that some cat or other has just knocked on the floor some kind of, oh, phial of Sèvres porcelain belonging to the grief-stricken princess or young noblewoman, or that it has torn into shreds some priceless peignoir or other. Would she be storming around, or flailing about with her hands? Of course not, because all that would have been nonsense to her, because for a day or three, she is 'more elevated' than any kind of peignoir or cat or Sèvres porcelain.

"So how is it? Is this princess boring? She is impossibly boring, that's certain. Is she frivolous? In the highest degree.

"Just like me. Now you know why I'm the saddest of sots, a lightweight among idiots and gloomier than any shitass? Why I'm a fool, a demon, and a bag of wind all at the same time?

"It's great that you've understood it all. Let's drink to understanding with what's left of the Kubanskaya, right from the bottle, and let's drink it straight down.

"This is how it's done . . ."

The rest of the Kubanskaya was still seething somewhere not far from my throat, so when the words *Why did you drink it all, Venya? That's too much* came from heaven, I was hardly able to breathe out in response: "In the whole world . . . in the whole world all the way from Moscow to Petushki there has never been anything like 'too much' for me. . . . And why are you fearful for me, heavenly angels?"

We fear that you're going . . .

"That I'm going to start swearing again? Oh, no, no, I simply didn't know that you were with me constantly or I wouldn't have before, either . . . Minute by minute I'm getting happier and if I start to get foul-mouthed, it's only because I'm happy. How silly you are."

No, we're not silly, we are only afraid that once again you won't get there.

"Won't get where? I won't get to Petushki? To her? To my shameless Tsaritsa with eyes like clouds? You're really funny."

No, we're not funny, we're afraid you won't get to him and he won't get any nuts.

"What do you mean? While I live . . . what do you mean? Last Friday, it's true, she wouldn't let me go to see him. Last Friday I went limp, angels, I took to staring at her white belly, round like the sky and the earth. But, today, I'll get there, if only I don't croak . . . killed by fate . . . today I'll be with her and I'll graze among the lilies till morning. But, tomorrow . . ."

The poor kid, the angels sighed.

" 'Poor kid?' Why 'poor'? Tell me, angels, you'll be with me right up to Petushki? You won't fly off?"

Oh, no, we can't ride as far as Petushki. We'll be flying off as soon as you smile. You haven't smiled once today. As soon as you smile for the first time, we're off.

"And there on the platform, you'll meet me, right?"

Yes, we'll meet you there.

"You're lovely creatures, angels. Only why that 'poor kid'? He's not a poor kid at all, the little one who knows the letter *Ю* like his own five fingers, the little one who loves his father as himself.

"OK, suppose he was sick the Friday before last and everyone there was afraid for him. But then, he got better, as soon as he saw me . . . Yes, yes . . . Gracious God, make it so that nothing has happened to him and so that nothing ever will.

"Make it, Lord, so that even if he has fallen from the roof or the stove he won't have broken either his arm or his leg. If he happens to see a knife or a razor, let him not play with them, Lord, please find other playthings for him, Lord. When his mother stokes the fire, which he loves to watch, drag him off to one side, if you can, Lord. It pains me to think that he might get burned. And if he should get sick, let him start getting better the minute he sees me."

Yes, when I arrived the last time, they told me he was asleep; he was sick and had a fever. I drank lemon vodka by his crib and they left me alone with him. He really did have a fever—even the dimple on his cheek was all warm, and it was curious that such a little nothing could have a fever.

I drank three glasses of lemon vodka before he woke up

49

and looked at me and my fourth glass, which I had in my hand. I talked with him for a long time, and said:

"You know what, kid? Don't die . . . think about it (after all you can already draw letters, so you can think for yourself). It's foolish to die, knowing only the letter $\mathscr{H}$ and nothing else . . . You understand that it's foolish?"

"I understand, Father . . ."

The way he said that. Everything they say—the eternally living angels and eternally dying children—is so important that I feel I should write down the words in flowing longhand, but I would write everything *we* say in tiny letters, because what we say is more or less nonsense. "I understand, Father."

"You'll get up again, kid, and dance around again to my 'Little Piggies' Farandole.' Do you remember? When you were two years old you danced to it. Music by father, and words, too. 'They're such little dears, such funny little devilkins, they snatched and scratched and bit my tummy.' And you danced like a tiny fool, one hand on your waist and waving a handkerchief in the other. 'Since Feb-ru-ary I whimpered and whined, and toward the end of August I turned up my toes.' Do you love your father, kid?"

"Very much."

"There, see, don't die. When you've not died and you get better, you'll dance something for me again. Only, we won't dance the farandole. It's got words that don't fit. 'Toward the end of August I turned up my toes.' That doesn't work. 'One, two, three, lay me down to sleep' would be much better."

I finished my fourth glass, and got upset:

"When you're not around, kid, I'm entirely alone. You

understand? You played in the woods this summer, right? And, probably, you remember the pines there? That's me, like a pine tree. It's very, very tall and very, very lonely, that's me too. It's like me, looking only into the sky, and whatever is underneath it doesn't see and doesn't want to see. It's green and will always be green until it tumbles down. That's me, too. Until I tumble down, I'll always be green."

"Green," the little one responded.

"Take the dandelion, for instance. It sways in the wind and scatters, and it's sad to look at it. That's me, too. I scatter in the wind. Isn't it disgusting to see how I scatter in the wind for days on end?"

"Disgusting," the little one repeated after me, and smiled blissfully.

Even now I remember his "disgusting" and I smile, also blissfully. And I see the angels nod at me from afar and fly away as they had promised.

KUCHINO—ZHELEZNODOROZHNAYA

But, first of all, I'll see her. First of all. To see her on the platform with her braid from head to tail, to blush and to burn and to get drunk lying on my back, and to graze among the lilies so that I die from sheer exhaustion.

> Bring bracelets and necklaces,
> I want to dress up like a queen,
> Silk and velvet, pearls and diamonds,
> For my king has come back to me.

This girl is more than a girl. She's a temptress, she's a ballad in A flat major. This woman, this red-haired bitch isn't a woman, she's a witch. You ask, "But, Venichka, where did you dig her up and where did she come from, this red-haired bitch? How can there be anything worthwhile in Petushki?"

"There can be," I say to you, and I'll say it so loud that Moscow and Petushki will tremble. Moscow, no, that couldn't happen with Moscow, but with Petushki it could. And what if she is a bitch? If you want to know where I dug her up, if you're interested, just listen, since you're so shameless, I'll tell you the whole story.

"As I told you before, in Petushki the jasmine never stops blooming and the birds always sing, so, exactly ten weeks ago today, the birds were singing and the jasmine was blooming. And it was also the birthday of someone or other. In addition, there was an endless stream of liquor, ten bottles or twelve or twenty-five. And there was anything anyone could wish for, from beer on tap to bottled stuff."

"And what else?" you ask, "and what else?"

"There were also two lads. And three young things getting drunk, one girl drunker than the next and all hell breaking loose. So I mixed some Rossiiskaya with Zhiguli beer and drank it and looked at the three of them and perceived something in them. Exactly what, I can't say, so I mixed up another drink and the more I perceived of that 'something' the more I mixed and drank and therefore the more sharply I perceived it.

"But a responding perception I felt only in one of them. Oh, the red lashes, longer than the hair on your heads. Oh, the innocent whites of her eyes. Oh, that whiteness. Oh, the bewitching, dove-like wings . . . "

"Is that you, Erofeev?" She leaned toward me slightly, blinking her lashes.

"Well, sure. Nobody but me."

(Oh, the intuitive creature, how did she guess?)

"I've read some of your stuff, and, you know, I never thought that anyone could get so much drivel onto half a hundred pages. It's beyond imagination."

"Beyond, come on!" Flattered, I mixed up another drink. "If you like, I'll do better, I'll get even more in next time."

And that's how it all got started. That's how oblivion began—a three-hour gap. What did I drink? What did I talk about? In what proportions did I mix up my drinks? Perhaps there wouldn't have been any gap if I hadn't mixed my drinks. But no matter what, I came to after three hours, and this is the position I was in when I came to—sitting at the table mixing a drink.

And the two of us were alone, she next to me, laughing at me like a child of paradise. I thought, "Unheard of. This is a woman whose bosom, to this day, has been seized only by presentiment. This is a woman who, until me, no one has so much as felt the pulse of. Oh, that blissful itch in the soul and all over."

And she got up and drank 100 more grams. She drank standing up with her head tossed back like a pianist. And, having drunk, she breathed out everything from inside her, everything that was holy in her, everything. And then she arched her back like an elegant bitch and started to make wild movements with her hips with such suppleness that I couldn't look at her without shuddering.

Of course you'll ask (you've no conscience so you'll

ask), "So what, then, Venichka? Did she?" What can I say? "Well, of course, she . . ." "Not much, she sure . . . She said straight out, 'I want you to embrace me masterfully with your right hand.' Ha, ha. 'Masterfully' and 'with your right hand!' I who had gotten to the point where I couldn't even touch her torso—I wanted to but I couldn't find it, much less embrace her masterfully.

" 'Oh, move your sloping sides,' I thought, mixing a drink. 'Move, enchantress. Move, Cleopatra, move your splendid body, whore, leaving the poet's heart weary. All that I have, I fling today upon the white altar of Aphrodite.' "

This is what I was thinking. But she laughed and went up to the table and gulped down another 150 grams, for she was perfection and perfection knows no bounds.

ZHELEZNODOROZHNAYA—CHERNOE

She gulped it down and threw off her dress. "If," I thought, "if after that she takes off the rest, the earth will shudder and the stones will sing."

But she said, "Well, now, Venichka, is it nice here with me?" And, crushed by desire, I awaited the fall, gasping for breath. I said to her, "I've lived exactly thirty years in the world . . . but never before have I seen any place as nice as this."

What was I to do next? Be tender in an insinuating way or crude in a captivating way? The devil knows, I never really understood how or when to approach a drunken girl. Up to this point—should I tell you?—up to this point I knew little about them, drunken or sober. Of course, I rushed after them in my thoughts, but the moment I would catch up, my heart would stop in fright. I had designs but not intentions. Whenever any intentions appeared my designs disappeared and, though I rushed after them in my heart, my thought stopped in fright. I was contradictory. On the one hand, I liked it that they had waists, while we haven't any waists at all. This awoke in me—how should I put it?—"bliss." Yes, it awoke a feeling of bliss in me. But, on the other hand, they stabbed Marat with a penknife, though Marat was incorruptible and shouldn't have been stabbed. This thought killed all feelings of bliss. On the other hand, like Karl Marx I liked the weakness in them, that is, for example, how they are compelled to squat down when urinating. This pleased me, this filled me with, well, with what? A feeling of bliss, really? Well, yes, this filled me with a feeling of bliss. But, on the other hand, didn't one of them shoot at Lenin? This killed the bliss again—squat away, but why shoot at Ilich? It would be strange to speak of bliss after that. . . . Now I've gotten distracted.

And so, what was I to do? Be threatening or captivating?

She herself made the choice for me, leaning back and stroking my cheek with her ankle. There was something like encouragement in this, something like the blowing of a kiss. And, then, that turbid, bitchy whiteness of her pupils, whiter than delirium, whiter than seventh heaven. And her stomach that was like the sky and the earth. As soon as I saw it I all but started to weep from inspiration, to tremble and steam all over. And everything got mixed together—roses and lilies and, in little tangles, the whole damp shuddering entrance to Eden and oblivion. Oh, the moist sobbing of those depths. Oh, the shamelessness of those eyes. Oh, harlot with eyes like clouds. Oh, sweet navel.

Everything got mixed together. And I know that today will be the same, the same intoxication and the same slaughter.

You'll say to me, "What do you think, Venichka, that you are the only slaughterer she's got?"

"And what is it to me? And to you all the more? Even if she isn't faithful, let her. Age and fidelity cause wrinkles, and I don't want her to have a wrinkled mug. Let her be unfaithful . . . not exactly 'let her,' of course, but, no matter, let her. You see, she's woven all from bliss and aromas. She's not one to be pawed or beaten . . . you've got to breathe her in. Once I tried to count all her innermost curves, and I couldn't. I counted up to twenty-seven and got so dizzy from faintness that I drank some Zubrovka and gave up counting.

"But more beautiful than anything are her forearms. Especially when she moves them, laughing ecstatically, and says, 'Eh, Erofeev, you sinful shitass.' Oh, the she-devil. Is it possible not to breathe in someone like her?"

She could also be venomous, but that was all nonsense, a form of self-defense and of something feminine—I understand very little about these things. In any case, when I had gotten to the core of her there was no venom left, just strawberries and cream. On one Friday, for instance, when I was really warm from the Zubrovka, I said to her:

"Come on, let's be together our whole life. I'll carry you off to Lobnya, clothe you in purple and linen, and make a little extra working on telephone boxes while you'll sit home sniffing something—lilies, let's say. Come on."

But silently she made a fig with her hand. Languidly, I drew it to my nostrils, breathed in, and started to cry:

"But why? Why?"

She made me another fig. I drew it in and frowned and started crying again:

"But why?" I implored. "Answer, why???"

And then she started sobbing and flopped onto my neck:

"Lunatic, madman, you know exactly why."

And since then almost every Friday the same thing has been repeated—the tears and the figs. But today, today, something will be decided because today is our thirteenth Friday. And I'm getting closer and closer to Petushki, Heavenly Queen. . . .

CHERNOE—KUPAVNA

I pace around in the vestibule, smoking the whole time.

"And you say that you're lonely and misunderstood? You who have so much in your soul and beyond it? You who have someone like that in Petushki? And someone like the one beyond Petushki? . . . Lonely?"

"No, no, I'm not lonely anymore, not misunderstood anymore. For twelve weeks I've been understood. All the past is gone. Why, I remember when I turned twenty—at that time, I was hopelessly lonely. And my birthday was a despondent one. Yuri Petrovich and Nina Vasilievna came, they brought me a bottle of Stolichnaya and a can of vegetable-stuffed cabbage, and I felt so lonely, so impossibly lonely, because of those cabbage rolls and the Stolichnaya so that, against my will, I started to cry.

"And when I turned thirty last fall? The day was dismal, like the day when I turned twenty. Borya came with some half-intelligent poetess, Vadya and Lida came, Ledik and Volodya. And they brought me? What? Two bottles of Stolichnaya and two cans of stuffed tomatoes. And such despair, such torment possessed me because of those tomatoes that I wanted to cry but now could not.

"Does this mean that in the course of those ten years I had become less lonely? No, it doesn't mean that. Does it mean that my soul had become coarsened in those ten years? And my heart hardened? It doesn't mean that either—more likely the opposite. But, all the same, I wanted to cry but couldn't.

"Why? Very likely I'll be able to explain that to you, if I can find some kind of analogy for it from the world of the beautiful. Let's say, for instance, a quiet person drinks 750 grams and becomes boisterous and full of joy. If he adds another 700, will he become even more boisterous and full of joy? No, he'll quiet down again. It'll even seem on the surface that he has sobered up. But does this mean that he has, in fact? Never happens. He's just gotten piggishly drunk and is quiet for that reason."

It is just the same with me. I did not become less lonely in those thirty years and my heart did not become calloused—quite the contrary. But if you look at it on the surface . . .

No, take now—to live and live. Living is not at all boring.

Only Nikolai Gogol was bored, and King Solomon. If we've already lived through thirty years, it's necessary to try to live another thirty. "Man is mortal." That's my opinion. But if we've already been born, there's nothing to be done about it, we must live for a little. . . . "Life is beautiful"—that's my opinion.

Really, do you know how many mysteries there are in the world, what an abyss of unstudied mysteries and what an expanse of space there is for those who draw these mysteries to themselves? Here is the simplest of examples:

What if yesterday you drank, let's say, 750 grams but in the morning it was unthinkable to be hung over—work and the like—and only long after midday, having suffered through six or seven hours, you finally have something to drink in order to ease your soul? (So, how much do you drink? Well, let's say, 150.) Why isn't your soul any easier? The queasiness which has accompanied you since morning, because of the 150 grams, has been replaced by a queasiness of a different category, a shy queasiness. Your cheeks get crimson like a whore's and under your eyes such blue appears as if the day before you hadn't drunk your 750 but had gotten your face kicked around instead. Why?

I'll tell you why. Because you have fallen victim to your six or seven hours at work. You have to have the ability to choose your work; there aren't any bad jobs or bad professions; one must respect every calling. It's necessary, just after waking, to drink something right away, or, no, I'm lying, not "something" but precisely the same thing that you were drinking the day before—and drink it every forty or forty-five minutes so that toward evening you have drunk 250 grams more than the day before. Then there won't be any queasiness or shyness and you will have such a white face it'll look as though it hasn't been kicked around for six months.

So you see how many puzzles there are in nature, how many blank spots everywhere.

But the empty-headed youth coming up to take our place doesn't seem to see the mysteries of existence. He lacks vision and initiative, and I doubt that he—that any of them—have any brains in their heads. What could be more noble, for example, than experimenting on oneself? At their age I would do this: on Thursday evening I'd drink, all at one go, three and a half liters of beer and vodka mixed. I'd drink it and lie down to sleep without getting undressed and with one thought only—will I wake up on Friday or won't I?

And, all the same, I wouldn't wake up on Friday. I'd wake up on Saturday and not in Moscow either but under the railroad embankment in the Naro-Fominsk region. And later, I would, with effort, recollect and gather the facts. And having gathered them, I'd put them together. And having put them together, I would start again to recreate by straining my memory with the most penetrating analysis. And, later, I'd go from observation to abstraction; in other words, thoughtfully I would have a morning-after drink and, finally, find out what had happened to Friday.

Ever since childhood, since thumb-sucking days, my favorite word has been "dare," and, as God is my witness, I took plenty of chances. If you took the chances

I did, you'd either bust your gut or have a stroke. Or, actually, if at your age you took the chances I did, one fine morning you'd wake up dead. But I woke up every morning and started taking chances again.

For example: approaching eighteen years of age, I noticed that from the first shot through the fifth I would ripen, but beginning with the sixth,

and on through the ninth, I would go soft. I'd go so soft that on the tenth I would have to shut my eyes. And what would I think in my naivete? I would think I must, by force of will, overcome the queasiness and drink the eleventh; then perhaps a return to maturity will occur. But, no, nothing. At this point I experienced no return.

I mulled this puzzle over for three years straight, I mulled it over daily and, all the same, I'd fall asleep after the tenth.

And actually it turned out to be so simple: if you've already drunk the fifth shot, you must drink the sixth, seventh, eighth, and ninth immediately, at one go, but drink them in an ideal sense—that is, drink them only in your imagination. In other words you must, by force of will alone, and at one go, not drink numbers six, seven, eight, and nine.

And having withstood the pause, take off directly on the tenth, just as with the ninth symphony of Dvořák, which is actually the ninth but conditionally called the fifth. The same with you—call your sixth your ninth and be sure that now you'll reach maturity without hindrance, and do so from the sixth (the ninth) up to and including the twenty-eighth (the thirty-second). That is, reach maturity to the point beyond which lie insanity and piggishness.

No, honestly, I despise the generation coming up to take our place. It inspires repulsion and terror in me. And don't think Maksim Gorky will sing songs about them. I don't say that at their age we dragged around with ourselves a whole load of that which is holy. Good Lord, no, sacred things touched us lightly, but on the other hand there were so many things on which we did not spit. But they, they spit on everything.

Why don't they take up—here's what: at their age I would drink, with large intervals. I'd drink and drink and stop drinking, drink and drink and again stop drinking. I've no right to judge therefore whether morning depression is more lively if you make it a daily habit, that is, if from age sixteen you drank 450 grams at seven in the evening. Of course, were my life to start over again, I would try it—but would they? Would they?

If only that. While how much uncertainty do other spheres of human life conceal within themselves! Just suppose, for example, that one day you drink ordinary vodka exclusively. But, the next day, other stuff exclusively. On the first day, toward midnight, you stop like one possessed. Toward midnight you burn so that the Ukrainian girls could jump over you as they jump over the bonfire on Ivan Kupalo Eve. It's quite clear they will make it over if you've drunk ordinary vodka exclusively.

But if you have drunk only other kinds from morning till night? Then the girls won't be jumping over you on Ivan Kupalo Eve. On the contrary, let a girl sit down on Ivan Kupalo Eve and you won't be able to jump over her. On the condition, of course, that you drank only the other stuff all day.

Yes, yes. But how much do experiments in narrow areas tell us? Take, for example, hiccuping, that is, the study of drunken hiccuping in its mathematical aspect.

"For goodness' sake," they cry from every side. "Really, isn't there anything else in the world besides that, isn't there anything which you could . . ."

I cry to all sides, "No. No, there is nothing. No, there's nothing else. . . . I'm no fool, I know that in this world there is also psychiatry, and extragalactic astronomy."

But, really, all that is not for us. All that was thrust on us by Peter the Great and Dimitri Kipalchich, the Decembrist astronomer, and really our calling is not here at all, our calling is in an entirely different direction. In the direction where I will take you if you're willing. You'll say, "This calling is vile and false." But I'll say to you, I'll repeat, "There are no false callings—respect is due everyone who toils."

And fie on you finally. Better to leave extragalactic astronomy to the Yanks and psychiatry to the Germans. Let all pigdom like the Spanish go to look at their corrida, let the scoundrel of an African build his Aswan Dam (all the same the wind will blow it away), let Italy choke on its idiotic bel canto, let . . .

But, I repeat, we shall take up hiccuping.

KILOMETER 33—ELECTROUGLI

In order to begin this investigation it goes without saying that it will be necessary to induce it either *an sich* (Immanuel Kant's term meaning "to induce it in yourself) or to induce it in another, but for your own reasons—that is, *für sich*. Best of all, of course, is to induce it both *an sich* and *für sich*, like so: drink something strong for two hours. Starka, Trapper's, or Hunter's vodka. Drink it in a large glass. If this is difficult for anyone, he may permit himself a small bite to eat, something unpretentious: a piece of not-very-fresh bread, spiced sprats, plain sprats, or sprats in tomato sauce. Then take an hour's break. But don't eat anything and don't drink anything; just let your muscles relax and don't exert yourself.

And you will be convinced—toward the end of the hour it will begin. When you hiccup the first time, you'll be astonished by its unexpectedness, then you'll be astonished by the inevitability of the second, third, fourth time, etc. But, if you are no fool, you'll soon stop being astonished and get to work. Write down on paper at what intervals your hiccups deign to honor you. In seconds, of course:

eight, thirteen, seven, three, eighteen.

Try to find here some kind of periodicity, albeit the most approximate; even if you're a fool, attempt to deduce any kind of an idiotic formula in order somehow to predict the length of the next interval, at least. No matter, life will overturn all your silly moods:

seventeen, three, four, seventeen, one, twenty, three, four, seven, seven, seven, eighteen.

They say that the leaders of the world proletariat, Karl Marx and Friedrich Engels, thoroughly studied the schema of social formulae and, on this basis, were able to foresee much. But here they would be powerless to foresee the least thing. You have entered, following your

64

own whim, into the sphere of the inevitable—be at peace and be patient. Life will disgrace both your elementary and your higher mathematics:

thirteen, fifteen, four, twelve, four, five, twenty-eight.

Is it not so with every individual's triumphs and failures, ecstasies and afflictions—isn't there the slightest hint of regularity? Is it not thus that the catastrophes in the life of humanity follow one another in confusion? Law is higher than us all. The hiccup is higher than any law. And as its onset so astonished us not long before, so its ending will astonish us, an ending which—like death—you can neither predict nor stave off:

twenty-two, fourteen—that's all, then silence.

And in this silence your heart says to you: It is indiscernible and we are helpless. We are deprived of freedom of will and are in the power of the arbitrary which has no name and from which there is no escape.

We are mere trembling creatures while it is omnipotent. It—that is, the Right Hand of God which is raised above us all and before which only cretins and rogues do not bow their heads. He is incomprehensible and, therefore, He is.

And thus, be perfect as your Heavenly Father is perfect.

ELEKTROUGLI—KILOMETER 43

Yes. Drink more, eat less. This is the best method of avoiding self-conceit and superficial atheism. Take a look at a hiccuping atheist: he is distracted and dark of visage, he suffers and he is ugly. Turn away from him, spit, and look at me when I begin to hiccup: a believer in overcom-

65

ing who is without any thought of rebellion, I believe in the fact that He is good and that therefore I myself am good.

He is good. He leads me from suffering toward the light. From Moscow toward Petushki. Through the torments of the Kursk Station. Through the purgation at Kuchino, through the fancies of Kupavna to the light of Petushki. *Durch leiden–licht.*

I paced about in the vestibule in even more terrible agitation. And kept on smoking. And here, a clear thought struck my brain like lightning.

What else am I to drink so that this exultation will not be extinguished? What am I to drink in Thy name?

Oh, misfortune! I have nothing that would be worthy of Thee. Kubanskaya, that's rot. While Rossiiskaya, it's ridiculous to speak of it in Thy presence. And stout red at one thirty-seven. God! . . .

No, if I get to Petushki unharmed today, I'll make a cocktail which it will be possible to drink without shame in the presence of God and man, in the presence of man and in the name of God. I'll call it "Jordan's Waters" or "The Star of Bethlehem." If I forget about that in Petushki, please remind me.

Don't laugh. I have vast experience in the creation of cocktails. From Moscow to Petushki people drink these cocktails not knowing the name of their creator. They drink the "Balsam of Canaan," they drink the "Tear of a Komsomol Girl" and it's right that they should do so. If it is true that we cannot wait to be favored by nature, we must wrest her favors from her, then it goes without saying that it is necessary to know exact recipes. If you wish, I'll give you these recipes. Listen.

To drink vodka, even from the bottle, is nothing other than weariness of spirit, and vanity. To mix vodka with eau de cologne, there is a certain caprice, but no pathos whatsoever. But if you drink a glass of "Balsam of Canaan," there is caprice and an idea and pathos, and beyond that a hint of the metaphysical.

Which component of "Balsam of Canaan" do we value above all else? Well, the methylated spirits, of course. But, after all, the methylated spirits, being only an object of inspiration, are themselves simply devoid of this inspiration. What is it, in this case, that we value in the methylated spirits even more? Of course, the naked taste sensation. And, even more than that, the miasma which it exudes. In order to set off this miasma, a touch of fragrance is necessary. For this reason velvet beer or, best of all, Ostankino or Czech beer, is added in the proportion 1:2, with one part refined furniture polish.

I won't remind you how to refine furniture polish—any child knows that. For some reason no one in Russia knows why Pushkin died, but how to refine furniture polish—that, everyone knows.

In any event, write down the recipe for "Balsam of Canaan" (as one of our hack writers might have put it, "Life is given to man only one time and it must be lived so as not to make mistakes in recipes"):

Methylated Spirits	100 g.
Velvet Beer	200 g.
Refined Furniture Polish	100 g.

And so you have before you "Balsam of Canaan." In plain speech it is called a Black Fox and the liquid is a blackish brown, of moderate strength and a staunch aroma that is really not an aroma, but a hymn. A hymn of democratic youth, because this cocktail fosters vulgarity and dark forces in the drinker. I've observed this many times! . . . And to stave off the fostering of these dark forces there are two means. First, not to drink "Balsam of Canaan" and, second, to drink in place of it the cocktail called "The Spirit of Geneva."

There's not a drop of nobility in "The Spirit of Geneva," but it does have bouquet. You'll ask, "What is the secret of its bouquet?" I'll answer you, "I don't know what the secret of its bouquet is." Then you'll give it some thought and ask, "So what is the key?" And the key to it lies in the fact that you shouldn't replace White Lilac eau de cologne with any other kind, not Jasmine, not Sweetbrier, not Lily of the Valley. "In the world of components there are no equivalents," as the old alchemists said, and they knew what they were talking about. That is, your Lily of the Valley Silver is not White Lilac even in the moral sense, not to speak of bouquet.

Lily of the Valley, for example, excites the mind, disturbs the conscience, strengthens a sense of one's inalienable rights. While White Lilac, on the other hand, soothes the conscience and reconciles man to the sore spots of life.

Once I drank a whole phial of Lily of the Valley Silver, sat down, and started crying. Why was I crying? Because I recalled my Mama, recalled her and couldn't forget her. "Mama," I say. And I cry. And then again, "Mama," I say, and once more I cry. Somebody else would have just sat there crying. But me? I grabbed a phial of Lilac and drank it. And what do you think? My tears dried up. And I was overcome by idiotic laughter, and as for Mama—I even forgot her name.

Therefore, how ridiculous someone preparing "The Spirit of Geneva" seems if he adds Lily of the Valley Silver to the athlete's foot remedy! Listen to the exact recipe:

White Lilac	50 g.
Athlete's Foot Remedy	50 g.
Zhiguli Beer	200 g.
Alcohol Varnish	150 g.

But if someone doesn't want to tramp the universe to no good purpose, let him send to the devil both "Balsam of Canaan" and "The Spirit of Geneva." He had better sit down at the table and prepare himself some "Tear of a Komsomol Girl." Odorous and strange is this cocktail. Why it is odorous, you'll find out later. I'll explain first why it is strange.

Somebody drinking just vodka will keep his right mind and a clear head or he'll lose them both at once. But in the case of a "Tear" it's funny—you drink 100 grams of this "Tear" and your head is clear and it's as if you never had a right mind. You drink 100 more grams and you'll be surprised at yourself. Where did all the right mind come from? And where did your clear head get to?

Even the "Tear"'s recipe itself is fragrant. And from the prepared cocktail, from its odorousness it is possible to lose consciousness for a moment. *I* did, for example.

Lavender Toilet Water	15 g.
Verbena	15 g.

Herbal Lotion	30 g.
Nail Polish	2 g.
Mouthwash	150 g.
Lemon Soda	150 g.

The mixture prepared this way must be stirred for twenty minutes with a sprig of honeysuckle. Some, it is true, maintain that in case of necessity it is permissible to substitute dodder for honeysuckle.

But this is both incorrect and criminal. Cut me up left and right, but you won't get me to stir it with dodder. The "Tear" I'll stir with honeysuckle. I simply die laughing when I see somebody stirring a "Tear" with dodder and not honeysuckle.

But enough of the "Tear." Now I present to you the last and the best.

"Labor's crown is its own supreme reward," as the poet said. In any event, I present to you the cocktail "Bitches' Brew," a beverage which overshadows all others. This is more than a beverage—it is the music of the spheres. What is the finest thing in the world? The struggle for the liberation of humanity. But even finer is this (write it down):

Zhiguli Beer	100 g.
"Sadko" Shampoo	30 g.
Dandruff Treatment	70 g.
Athlete's Foot Remedy	30 g.
Small Bug Killer	20 g.

The whole thing is steeped for a week in cigar tobacco and served at table.

I have received letters, incidentally, in which idle

readers have recommended one more thing: that the infusion obtained in the above fashion should be run through a colander, i.e., run it through and go to bed. All these supplements and corrections come from flabbiness of imagination, from an insufficiency of mental scope; that's where these absurd corrections come from.

"Bitches' Brew" can be served at table and should be drunk with the appearance of the first star, in large gulps. After only two goblets of this cocktail, a person will become so inspired that it is possible to go up to him for half an hour and, standing one and a half meters away, spit in his fat face without his saying a thing.

KILOMETER 43—KHRAPUNOVO

Did you at least manage to write down something? In Petushki, I promise to share with you the secret of "Jordan's Waters," if I get there alive, if God is gracious.

But now let us think about what I'm to drink next? What sort of a combination can I create out of the junk that's left in my suitcase? "Aunt Clara's Kiss?" Maybe. I won't be able to squeeze any other kind of kisses out of the thing, except "First Kiss" and "Aunt Clara's Kiss." Should I explain to you what a "Kiss" is? A "Kiss" means any red wine mixed fifty-fifty with any vodka. Let's take dry grape plus pepper vodka or Kubanskaya—that's a "First Kiss." A mix of homebrew and port wine Number Thirty-three—that's a "Forced Kiss" or, more simply, a "Cold Kiss" or, more simply, "Lenin's Lady." There are quite a few of the various "Kisses." In order not to feel like throwing up from all these "Kisses" it is necessary to get used to them from childhood.

71

I've got Kubanskaya in my suitcase. But no dry grape. Which means that a "First Kiss" is out of the question for me; I can only dream of one. But I do have about one and a half quarter bottles of Rossiiskaya and the stout rosé at a rub' thirty-seven. Together they would make us an "Aunt Clara's Kiss." I agree with you—its taste properties are plain and it is nauseating in the highest degree, but what's to be done if there isn't any dry wine? It will simply be necessary to drink "Aunt Clara's Kiss."

I went back into the car in order to mix my junk up into a "Kiss." Oh, it's been so long since I was here last, since I got out at Nikolskoe. As last time, dozens of eyes looked at me, big eyes ready for anything . . . slipping out of orbit, my homeland was looking me in the eye. Before, after the 150 grams of Rossiiskaya, those eyes pleased me. Now, after 500 grams of Kubanskaya, I was in love with those eyes, in love like a madman. I all but lurched into the car, though I went over toward my bench quite independently and, just in case, smiling slightly.

I went over to it and was dumbstruck. Where is my quarter bottle of Rossiiskaya, where is the very quarter bottle which, at Hammer & Sickle, I had finished only half of? Right from Hammer & Sickle it had stood by my suitcase with almost 100 grams left in it—where is it now?

I looked them all over but no one batted an eyelash. No, I'm positively in love and I'm crazy. Where did the angels fly off to? They were looking after the suitcase in my absence—when did they fly off? In the Kuchino region? Right. That means that it was stolen between Kuchino and Kilometer 43. While I was sharing with you the ecstasy of my feelings, while I was initiating you into the secrets of being, I was being deprived of my "Aunt Clara's Kiss." In the simplicity of my soul, I did not once look into the car all that time. . . . But now "enough of simplicity," as the dramatist Ostrovsky put it. And *finita la comedia*. Not all simplicity is holy. And not every comedy is divine . . . Enough of fishing in muddy water, it's time to be a fisher of men.

But how and whom?

The devil knows in which guise I'll arrive in Petushki. All the way from Moscow it was memoirs and philosophical essays, it was all poems in prose, as with Ivan Turgenev. Now the detective story begins. I took a look inside my suitcase: is everything there? Everything was there. But where is the 100 grams? And whom do I accuse?

I glanced to the right—the same pair is still sitting there, the stupid one and the intelligent one. The stupid one in the quilt jacket has long since gotten tipsy and fallen asleep. The intelligent one in the worsted overcoat is sitting opposite him, trying to wake him up. He is going about it as if he were trying to skin the stupid one alive: he takes him by a button and jerks him as far as he can toward himself, as if drawing a bowstring, and then lets him go. And the stupid one flies back and buries himself into the back of the bench like Cupid's dull arrow into the heart.

"Tran-scen-den-tal," I thought. Has he been at it for a long time? No, these two couldn't have stolen it. One of them is wearing a quilt jacket, it's true, and the other one isn't sleeping, so in principle either of them could have. But then, one is sleeping and the other is wearing a worsted overcoat . . . so neither one could have stolen it.

I glanced back—no, there's nothing there which would suggest . . . Indeed, two people do suggest something, but not these two. Very strange, this man and woman. They are sitting on different sides of the car at opposite windows and obviously are not acquainted. But for all that, they look amazingly similar—he is wearing a jacket and she is wearing a jacket; he has a brown beret and a black moustache, she has a brown beret and a black moustache.

I rubbed my eyes and looked back once again. An amazing resemblance, and each was incessantly looking the other over, angrily. It's clear they could not have stolen the 100 grams.

And ahead? I looked ahead.

Ahead, another strange pair: a grandfather and his grandson. The grandson is two heads taller than his grandfather and feebleminded probably from birth. The grandfather is two heads shorter but feebleminded, too. Both look me straight in the eye and lick their lips.

"Suspicious," I thought. Why is it they're licking their lips? Everyone else is looking me in the eye too, but no one else is licking his lips. Very suspicious. I started to look them over as intently as they were looking at me.

No, the grandson is a complete cretin. Even his neck is abnormal; it doesn't grow into his torso, it grows out of it, rising toward the back of his head together with the collarbones. And he breathes idiotically: first he exhales, then he inhales, when with everyone else it's the opposite—first inhaling and only then exhaling. And he looks at me, his eyes gaping and his mouth screwed up.

But the grandfather—he looked at me even more intensely, as if into the muzzle of a gun. And with such blue, swollen eyes that from both of these eyes moisture flowed—as from two drowned men—straight onto his boots. And he was like a man condemned to be shot, with a deathly pallor on his bald head. And his whole physiognomy was pockmarked as if he had been shot point-blank. In the middle of his shot face dangled a swollen, bluish nose that swayed like a victim of hanging.

"Verrry suspicious," I thought once more. And, rising from my place, I motioned with my finger for them to come here.

They both jumped up at once and rushed toward me, licking their lips the while. "This is also suspicious," I thought. "It seems to me they jumped up even a little before I motioned to them."

I invited them to sit down opposite me.

They both sat down, staring intently at my suitcase. The grandson was seated in a strange way—we all sit on our rear ends, but this one was somehow rolled on his left rib and seeming to offer one leg to me and the other to his grandfather.

"What's your name, Gramp, and where are you going?"

KHRAPUNOVO—ESINO

"I'm called Mitrich. And this is my grandson, he's also Mitrich. . . . We're going to Orekhovo, to the park, to ride the carousel. . . ."

And the grandson added: "E-e-e-e-e."

This sound was unusual and so devilishly offensive that I cannot reproduce it properly. He didn't speak, but rather squealed, with his left nostril and with great effort, as if he were raising the left nostril up with the right: "E-e-e-e-e, how fast we're traveling to Petushki, the renowned Petushki. E-e-e-e, what a drunk of a grandpa, what a good grandpa."

"So-o-o-o, you're going to ride the carousel."

"The carousel."

"Or, maybe not the carousel, after all?"

"The carousel," Mitrich asserted once more in the very same doomed voice, and moisture went on flowing from his eyes.

"But tell me, Mitrich, what did you do in here while I was out in the vestibule? While I was sunk in my own thoughts out there, in my own thoughts about my own feeling for a beloved woman? Hmmm? Tell me . . ."

Mitrich, not budging, somehow started to fidget.

No-nothing. I simply wanted to eat compote, compote with white bread."

"Compote with white bread?"

"Compote with white bread."

"Great. So, I'm standing in the vestibule all sunk in my thoughts about my feelings. And you, meanwhile, are searching my bench for compote with white bread. And not finding any compote . . ."

The grandfather broke down first and burst into tears, and the grandson after him. His upper lip entirely disappeared, while his lower one dangled down. Both cried.

"I understand you. Yes. I can understand everything. If I feel like forgiving you . . .I've got a soul the size of the Trojan horse's belly; it'll hold a lot. I forgive everything . . . if I feel like understanding, I understand—you just wanted compote with white bread. But you didn't find one or the other on my bench. And you were simply impelled to drink whatever you found there in place of that which you wanted."

I crushed them with my evidence. They both covered their faces and rocked contritely back and forth on the bench in time with my accusations.

"You remind me of a little old man in Petushki. He, too, drank only other people's stuff, he drank only stolen stuff. He'd lift a bottle of Triple eau de cologne from the pharmacy, go into the toilet at the station, and drink it on the sly. He called this drinking *Bruderschaft;* he was seriously convinced that this was drinking *Bruderschaft* and he died like that, in his delusion. So, what's up? Didn't you decide to drink *Bruderschaft?*"

They rocked back and forth and cried, and the grandson even started to blink with grief.

"But enough of tears. If I feel like understanding, I'll take it all in. I've got a head for indulgence. If you like, I can offer you some more. Each of you has already had 50 grams. I can give you another 50."

At that moment, someone came up from behind and said, "I want to drink with you, too."

Everyone looked at him at once. It was the man with the black moustache, the jacket, and the brown beret.

"E-e-e-e-e," young Mitrich started to squeal, "what a guy, what a tricky guy."

The man with the black moustache cut him short with a look, and, from beneath his moustache: "I am not tricky in any way. I don't steal like some. I don't steal the essentials of life from strangers. I've got my own—here."

And he set a bottle of Stolichnaya on the bench.

"You won't refuse some of mine?" he asked me.

I squeezed over to give him a place.

"No, but I'll have it later. Meanwhile, I'd like my own stuff, 'Aunt Clara's Kiss.' "

"Aunt Clara's?"

"Aunt Clara's."

We poured ourselves each his own stuff. Grandad and grandson waited for theirs—it turns out they were ready for it before I beckoned to them. Grandad pulled out the empty quarter bottle; I recognized it at once. And grandson pulled out a whole pitcher, pulled it out from somewhere between his pelvis and his diaphragm.

I poured them out what I had promised and they smiled.

"*Bruderschaft*, boys."

"*Bruderschaft*."

Everyone drank, throwing back their heads like pianists.

"This train does not stop at Esino. Stops at all points except Esino."

ESINO—FRIAZEVO

A rustling and a smacking of lips started up, as if the pianist, who had been drinking everything, had now drunk it all up and had then started to play Franz Liszt's Rhapsody in C sharp minor.

The first to speak was the man with the black moustache and the jacket. And, for some reason, he addressed himself only to me:

"I've read in Ivan Bunin that red-haired people, if they drink, always get red in the face."

"Well, what of it?"

"Whadaya mean 'what of it'? The last words of Anton Chekhov before he died were what? You remember? He said, *'Ich sterbe,'* that is, 'I'm dying.' And later he added, 'Pour me some champagne.' And only then did he die."

"So, so?"

"And Friedrich Schiller not only couldn't die, he couldn't live, without champagne. Do you know how he wrote? He'd put his feet in an icy bath, pour out the champagne, and write. He'd go through one glassful—and a whole act of a tragedy would be ready. He'd go through five glasses and a whole tragedy in five acts would be ready."

"So, so, so . . . Well, then . . ."

He cast ideas into me like the triumphant warrior tosses gold pieces, and I was barely able to pick them up.

"What about Nikolai Gogol?"

"What about him?"

"Whenever he was at the Panaevs he would always ask that they put a special pink goblet on the table."

"And did he drink out of the pink goblet?"

"Yes, he drank out of the pink goblet."

"And what did he drink?"

"Who knows? . . ."

"Well, what can you drink from a pink goblet? Vodka, naturally.

Both the Mitriches and I followed him with interest while he, the man with the black moustache, just laughed in anticipation of new triumphs.

"And old Modest Mussorgsky. My good God, do you know how he wrote his immortal opera *Khovanshchina?* It's laughter and grief. Modest Mussorgsky lies dead drunk in a ditch, and Nikolai Rimsky-Korsakov comes by dressed in a smoking jacket and carrying a bamboo walking stick. Nikolai Rimsky-Korsakov stops, tickles Modest with his walking stick and says, "Get up. Go wash yourself and sit down and finish your divine opera *Khovanshchina!*

"And so they sit there—Nikolai Rimsky-Korsakov in an armchair, crossing one leg over the other and with his top hat in his outstretched hand. While opposite him sits Modest Mussorgsky all limp, unshaven, hunched over a bench, sweating, writing down notes. Modest on the bench wants to tie one on—who cares about notes. But Nikolai Rimsky-Korsakov, with top hat in his outstretched hand, won't let him.

"But as soon as the door closes behind Rimsky-Korsakov, Modest gives up his immortal opera *Khovanshchina,* and it's thump—back into the ditch. And later he gets up and ties one on again and, again—thump . . .

"Well-read dev-v-v-il," old Mitrich interrupted him, enraptured.

"Yes, yes. I really love to read. There are so many fine books in the world," the man in the jacket continued. "For example, I drink for one month, for another, and then I read some book or other and how good it seems to me, this book, and so bad do I seem to myself that I get thoroughly upset that I can't read, then I give it up and start drinking. I drink for one month, then another, and then . . ."

"Wait a minute." Here it was I who interrupted him. "Wait. What about the Social Democrats?"

"What Social Democrats? Is it only the Social Democrats? All worthwhile people in Russia, all the necessary people, they all drank, they drank like pigs. But the superfluous, the muddle-headed ones, they didn't drink. Eugene Onegin, when he visited the Larins, the only thing he drank was bilberry juice, and that got him the trots. But Onegin's honest contemporaries 'between the Lafite and the Cliquot' were at that time giving birth to the 'mutinous science' and Decembrism . . . And when they finally awakened Herzen . . ."

"Hold it. Go ahead and wake him up, your Herzen," someone on the right bellowed suddenly. We gave a start and turned to the right. It was the cupid in the worsted overcoat. "This Herzen, he was supposed to get off at Khrapunovo, but he's still riding, the dog . . ."

Everyone who could laugh burst out laughing: "Ah, leave him in peace, the devil, Dick Decembrist." "Nothing between the ears." "What's the difference, Khrapunovo or Petushki. What if the old boy has taken it into his head to go to Petushki and you're throwing him off in Khrapunovo." Now everyone was getting imperceptibly tipsy, imperceptibly and joyously tipsy, imperceptibly and hideously . . . And me along with them.

I turned to the man in the jacket with the black moustache:

"Let's suppose they awakened Alexander Herzen. Just what have Democrats and *Khovanshchina* got to do with it?"

"Here's what! The whole thing got started from that rotgut instead of Clinquot—Democratization got started, the uproar and the *Khovanshchinas*. All your Ouspenskys, all your Pomialovskys—they couldn't write a line without a glass. I've read it, I know. They drank desperately. All the honest men of Russia. And why did they drink? They drank in desperation. They drank because they were honest, because they were not up to lightening the burden of the people. The people were suffocating in poverty and ignorance. Read Dmitri Pisarev. He writes the same thing: 'The people cannot permit themselves beef, but vodka is cheaper than beef, so the Russian peasant drinks because of his poverty. They cannot permit themselves a book, because at the marketplace there is neither Gogol nor Belinsky—just vodka, both government vodka and other kinds, and from the barrel, and to take home. Therefore he drinks, because of his ignorance he drinks.'

"How is one not to give way to despair, how not to write about the muzhik, how not to want to save him, how not to drink from despair? The Social Democrat writes books and drinks, he drinks as well as he writes. But the muzhik does not read and drink, he drinks without reading. Then Ospensky gets up and hangs himself and Pomialovsky lies down under a bench in a tavern and breathes his last and Garshin gets up and, dead drunk, throws himself over the railing."

The man in the black moustache had already gotten up and taken off his beret and was gesticulating like a madman. Everything he had drunk was stirring him up and rushing to his head, rushing, everything rushing. The Decembrist in the worsted overcoat—he gave up on his Herzen, sat down closer to us, and turned his uplifted, dull, damp eyes to the orator.

"You must look at what's happening! The darkness of ignorance is ever thickening, and impoverishment is growing. Have you read Marx? Everyone is drinking more and more. The Social Democrat's despair grows proportionally, now it's not Lafite or Cliquot—they somehow succeeded in awakening Herzen. But now all thinking Russia, grieving over the muzhik, drinks and never wakes up. Ring all the bells of London—no one in Russia will raise his head, everyone's lying in vomit, and life is hard for everyone.

"And so it is to this day. To this very day. This circle, this vicious circle of existence, it has me by the balls. I've only got to read a good book and I can't figure out who drinks for what reasons. The dregs looking up or the bigwigs looking down. Then, I can't go on, I drop the book. I drink for a month, for another, then . . ."

"Stop," the Decembrist interrupted him. "Is it really impossible not to drink? To take oneself in hand and not drink? Take the Privy Counselor Goethe, for example, he did not drink at all."

"Didn't drink? At all?" The man with the black moustache stood up and put on his beret. "That can't be."

"Oh, yes, it can. The man was able to take himself in hand and did not drink a single gram."

"You're speaking of Johann von Goethe?"

"Yes. I'm speaking of Johann von Goethe, who did not drink a single gram."

"Strange . . . And what if Friedrich Schiller had served him something? A goblet of champagne?"

"All the same he wouldn't have taken it. He would have taken himself in hand and not taken it. He would have said, 'I don't drink a gram.' "

The man with the black moustache was crestfallen and he started to grieve. His entire system had collapsed in public view, this system he had constructed by an ardent and brilliant stretching of points. "Help him, Erofeev," I

83

whispered to myself, "help the man. Any kind of blather, an allegory, a . . ."

"So you say that Privy Counselor Goethe did not drink a gram?" I turned to the Decembrist. "And why didn't he drink, do you know? What caused him not to drink? All honest minds drank but he did not? Why? Here we are going to Petushki and for some reason we stop everywhere except Esino. Why not stop at Esino too? But we don't. We barreled through without a stop. And it's all because there weren't any passengers in Esino. They all got on either at Khrapunovo or Friazevo. Right. They walked all the way from Esino itself as far as Khrapunovo or Friazevo and got on there. Because, all the same, the train is going to shoot through without a stop. So this is how Johann von Goethe acted, the old fool. Do you think he didn't want to drink? Of course he wanted to. But in order not to kick the bucket he forced all his characters to drink, instead. Take even his *Faust*. Who drinks in it? Everyone does. Faust drinks and gets younger. Siebel drinks and crawls all over Faust. Mephistopheles doesn't do anything but drink and treat the Krauts and sing "The Song of the Flea" to them. You ask, why was this necessary for Privy Counselor Goethe? And why did he force Werther to put a bullet in his forehead? Because—and there is proof—he himself was on the verge of suicide, but in order to shake off the temptation he forced Werther to do it, instead. You understand? He remained alive but it was as if he had committed suicide. And now was completely satisfied. This is even worse than real suicide. In this there is more cowardice and egoism.

"So, that's how your Privy Counselor drank, the same way he shot himself. Mephistopheles would take a drink and he'd be OK, the old cur. Faust would pour himself some more and—the old dork—he wouldn't be able to see straight. This old boy Nick worked with me on road construction—he, too, didn't drink. He was afraid that he'd drink a little and take off on a spree for a week, or for a month. But the rest of us, he all but forced us. He'd pour us something, grunt for us, get happy, the scum, and walk around as if he were in a stupor.

"The same goes for your vaunted Johann von Goethe. Schiller would serve him something, but he would refuse—and how. He was an alcoholic, he was an alky, your Privy Counselor, Johann von Goethe, and his hands shook, as it were."

"So that's it." The Decembrist and the man with the black moustache looked me over. The harmonious system was reestablished and, with it, gaiety. With a broad gesture, the Decembrist dragged a bottle of pepper vodka out of his worsted overcoat and placed it at the feet of the man with the black moustache. The man with the black moustache pulled out his Stolichnaya. Everyone rubbed their hands, agitatedly.

They poured me more than anyone. They also gave old Mitrich something and they gave a glassful to the young one, who clasped it happily to his left nipple with his right thigh, tears gushing from both nostrils.

"And so, to the health of Privy Counselor Johann von Goethe?"

"Yes, to the health of Privy Counselor Johann von Goethe."

As soon as I had finished drinking I felt that I was getting drunk beyond measure—and all the others, too.

"But . . . permit me to ask one trifling question," the man with the black moustache said through his moustache, and through the sandwich in his moustache. Again he addressed only me:

"Permit me to ask why it is you have so much sadness in your eyes? How can you be sad when you have so much knowledge? You'd think you haven't drunk anything since morning."

I was offended. "What do you mean, nothing? And is it really sadness? This is just bleariness. I'm just a little high."

"No, no, this bleariness is from sadness! You're like Goethe. You refute with your whole appearance a premise of mine, a speculative premise, but one growing out of experience. Like Goethe you refute everything."

"And how do I refute everything? With my bleariness?"

"Precisely. With your bleariness. Just listen to the point of my most cherished premise: When we drink in the evening and don't drink in the morning, what are we in the evening and what do we become the next morning? For example, if I drink, I'm devilishly merry—I have great mobility and I'm turbulent and I can't find a place for myself. But the next morning? The next morning I'm not simply not merry, not simply immobile, no. I am exactly as much gloomier than my normal self, my sober self, as I was merrier than my usual self the night before. If I was possessed by Eros the night before, then my morning revulsion to that is exactly equal to the dreams of the evening before. What do I want to say? Here, take a look." And the man with the black moustache depicted this silly theory. He explained that the horizontal line is the line of normal sober condition, the everyday line. The highest point of the curve is the moment of falling asleep, the lowest point, that of awakening with a hangover:

"You see, it's a pure mirror image. Stupid, stupid nature, she worries about nothing so zealously as she does about equilibrium. I don't know whether this worrying of hers is morally correct, but it *is* geometric. Look, this curve represents for us not only the vital spirit of life—it represents everything. In the evening, fearlessness—even if there's a reason to be afraid—we're fearless and under-estimate all values. While in the morning we overestimate all values and start getting afraid completely without reason.

"If of an evening's drinking nature has overpaid us, the next morning she shortchanges us with mathematical accuracy. If you had an urge for the ideal in the evening, let's say, your hangover will bring a rush of the anti-ideal. But if the ideal remains, then it will call forth an anti-rush. There in two words is my sacred premise.

"It is universal and applicable to everyone. But with you, it's not like with other people, it's like Goethe."

I laughed. "Why is it a premise then and not a postulate, if it's universal?"

And the Decembrist also laughed. "Be it universal, then, how come it's a premise?"

"Because it is. Because it does not take woman into account. It does take man as such into account, but not the ladies. With the appearance of a woman all mirror images are disrupted. If women weren't women, then the premise would not be a premise. The premise is universal so long as there aren't any women. With women the premise is no more. In particular if a woman is bad and the premise is a good one . . ."

Everyone started talking at once. "And what's a premise anyway?" "And what's a bad woman?" "There aren't any bad women, only a premise can be bad."

"I, for example," the Decembrist said, "I have thirty women, and every one is as good as the next, though I haven't a moustache. While you, let's say, have a moustache and only one good one . . . Even so, I consider thirty of the worst women to be better than one, even the best kind."

"What's the moustache got to do with it? We were talking about women, not moustaches."

"About moustaches, too. If it weren't for moustaches there wouldn't have been any talk."

"The devil knows what drivel you're blabbing . . . All the same, I think that one good one is worth all yours. How do *you* look at it?" The man with the black moustache again turned to me. "From the scientific point of view, how do you look at it?"

I said, "From the scientific point of view, of course, she is. In Petushki, for example, they give you one bottle of Trapper's for thirty empties, and if you bring in . . ."

"What! One for thirty? Why so many?" The hubbub started up again.

"Nobody else does it differently! Thirty empties at twelve kopeks, that's 3.60. And Trapper's costs 2.62. Any child knows that. They still don't know how Pushkin died, but that they know. You don't take any change because there's a good woman behind the counter, and you've got to humor a good woman."

"Yeah, what's so good about her, this woman behind the counter?"

"She's good in that a bad woman wouldn't have taken the bottles at all. But the good one takes bad bottles and gives you a good one. And, therefore, it is necessary to humor her. Come to think of it, what was woman placed on earth for?"

They all observed a significant silence. Each thought his own thoughts, or they all thought the same thing, for all I know.

"But how do you humor her? What did Maksim Gorky say on the Isle of Capri? 'The measure of any civilization is its way of relating to women.' Me, too. I go into the store in Petushki. I've got thirty empties with me. I say, 'Dearie,' in a voice which is so sad and so soused. I say, 'Be so kind, give me a bottle of Trapper's.' And really I know that I'm giving away almost a ruble: 3.60 minus 2.62. It's a pity. But she looks at me: should I give him the change, the scum, or not? And I look at her: will she give me the change, the slut, or not? Rather, no, at this moment I don't look at her. I look through her and beyond. And what arises before my meaningless gaze? Capri does. The agaves and the tamarinds, and underneath them sits

Maksim Gorky, hairy feet sticking out of white pants. And he threatens me with his finger: 'Don't take the change! Don't take the change!' I wink at him: 'Suppose there won't be anything to put in my mouth? Well, OK, I'll get something to drink but what'll I eat?'

"And he says: 'It's nothing, Venichka, you'll survive. And should you wish to eat, don't drink.' So I go out without the change. I'm angry of course, I think: 'The measure of civilization.' Ah, Maksim Gorky, you maxim of a Gorky, from stupidity or booze you blathered the like on your Isle of Capri? You're OK there, you'll gorge on your agaves, but what about me?"

They all laughed. And the grandson squealed, "E-e-e-e-e, what agaves, what a lovely Isle of Crappery . . ."

"And the bad woman?" said the Decembrist. "Doesn't it happen that the bad woman is really necessary too?"

"Of course, of course she is," I answered him. It happens that a bad woman sometimes is positively necessary to a good man. Take me, for example: twelve weeks ago I was in a coffin, I had been in a coffin for four years already, so that I had already stopped stinking. And they said to her, 'Look, he's in a coffin. Resurrect him, if you can.' And she walks up to the coffin, if only you had seen how she walks up to it."

"We know," said the Decembrist. "Walks the same as you write and you can't write worth shit."

"Right, right. She walked up to the coffin and she says, 'Talife cumi,' which means, in the translation from the Ancient Kike-ish: 'I say to you get up and walk.' And what do you think? I got up and walked. And it's already three months that I've been walking around, muddled as I am."

"Muddled from grief," the man with the black moustache and the little beret repeated. "And grief is from woman."

"He's muddled because he's been hitting the bottle," the Decembrist interrupted him.

"What's 'hitting the bottle' got to do with it, and why'd he 'hit the bottle'? Because, let's suppose a man grieves and goes to a woman. It's impossible to go to a woman and not drink. If you do, she's a bad one. Yes, even if she's a bad one, you've got to drink. In fact, the worse the woman, the more you've got to hit the bottle."

"Honestly," the Decembrist cried, "how marvelous it is that we're all so intelligent. We're just like in Turgenev—everyone sits around arguing about love. If you will, I'll tell you someting about an exceptional love and about how necessary bad women can be. Like in Turgenev, let's everyone tell something."

"Let's."

"Let's like in Turgenev."

Even old Mitrich, even he said, "Let's."

KILOMETER 61—KILOMETER 65

The Decembrist started to tell his story first.

"I had a friend, I'll never forget him. He was always kind of obsessed, but once nothing else but something like a demon possessed him. He went crazy over—you know what? Over Olga Erdeli, the renowned Soviet harpist. It could just as well have been Vera Dolova, she's also a renowned harpist. But it was this Erdeli he actually went crazy over. And not once in his life did he ever see her, he only heard on the radio how she strummed the harp and,

91

wouldn't you know, he went crazy over her.

"Went crazy and lay around. He didn't go to work, didn't study, didn't smoke, didn't drink, didn't get out of bed, didn't love the girls and didn't stick his head out the window. 'I'll take my pleasure with Olga Erdeli,' he'd say, 'and only then will I be resurrected. I'll get out of bed, I'll work and study, I'll drink and smoke and stick my head out the window.' And we'd say to him:

" 'So why Erdeli in particular? Take Vera Dolova, if you like, in place of Erdeli, Vera Dulova plays beautifully.'

"But he'd say, 'Go stuff your Vera Dulova! She's fit for a coffin, your Vera Dulova. I wouldn't sit down next to your Vera Dulova to take a crap!'

"So, we see that the kid is going to boil away completely. About three days later we go up to him again.

" 'How's it going, still raving about Olga Erdeli? We've found some medicine for you. If you want, we'll drag in Vera Dulova with a harp string for you tomorrow.'

" 'Sure,' he says, 'if you want me to strangle her with a harp string, go ahead and drag her in. I'll strangle her.'

"So what could we do? The kid was simply dying away, we had to save him. I went off to see Olga Erdeli, wanting to explain to her what was what, but I couldn't bring myself to do it. I even wanted to see Vera Dulova, but, no, I thought, he'll strangle her like a forget-me-not. I'm walking through Moscow in the evening and I'm sad; they're sitting there on their harps, playing, getting fat, while there's nothing left of the kid but ruins and ashes.

"And here I meet this hag of a woman, not so very old, but drunk as they come. 'A ruble, give me a rrrub'e,' she says. And just then it dawned on me. I gave her a ruble and explained everything. And she, this crone, turned out to be quicker than Olga Erdeli and, to make it all the more persuasive, I had her take a balalaika with her.

"And so, I dragged her off to my friend. We went in; he's lying down grieving as usual. I tossed him the balalaika, right from the threshold. And then shoved this Olga in his face; I let him have it with this Olga. 'Here she is—Erdeli! If you don't believe me, just ask.'

"And in the morning I take a look. The window is open, he had stuck his head out of it and had started smoking a bit. Then he started working a bit, studying, drinking . . . And he became a man like any other. So, you see . . ."

"Yeah, where's the love and where's Turgenev?" We all started up, hardly giving him a chance to finish. "No, go on about love. Have you read Ivan Turgenev? Well, if you have, tell us about it. Tell us about 'First Love,' about Zinochka, the heroine, about the veil and how they go to it with a whip on your ugly face—so, tell us about all that."

"Of course," I added, "in Turgenev it's a little bit different, in Turgenev they all get together around the hearth, in top hats, holding jabots in outstretched hands. Oh well, OK, even without the hearth we've got something to warm up with. And what do we need with jabots? Even without the jabot we can't see straight."

"Of course, of course."

"If one is to love à la Turgenev, that means to be able to sacrifice everything for the sake of a chosen creature. To be able to do what is impossible to do while not loving à la Turgenev. Take you, old buddy [We had started imperceptibly to get really friendly with each other.] Take you,

Decembrist. This friend you told us about, would you be able to bite off one of his fingers for the sake of a beloved woman?"

"Why a finger? What's a finger got to do with it?" the Decembrist groaned.

"No, no. Listen. So could you, at night, creep into the party office, take off your pants and drink a whole bottle of ink, then put the bottle back, put on your pants and quietly return home? For the sake of a beloved woman? Could you?"

"My God, no, I couldn't."

"So, there you are."

"But *I* could," Grandad Mitrich spoke up suddenly. "But I could tell you a little something."

"You? What? You've probably never even read Ivan Turgenev."

"Well, so what if I haven't . . . My grandson, he's read everything."

"Then we'll give your grandson the floor later. Go on, Gramps, tell us about love!"

"I can imagine," I thought, "what drivel this'll be, what unmitigated drivel." And I suddenly remembered my boast on the day I met my Tsaritsa: "I'll put in even more rubbish next time. Even more." So, what? Let him talk, this Mitrich with the runny eyes. We must honor, I repeat, the dark reaches of another's soul. We must look into them even if there's nothing there, even if there's only trash there. It's all one; look and honor it, look and don't spit on it.

Grandad started to tell his story:

"We had a chairman—he was called Lohengrin—really strict and all covered with boils . . . and he'd go out every night for a motorboat ride and steer out onto the river . . . and squeeze his boils . . ."

Moisture flowed from Grandad's eyes. He was excited.

"He'd have his ride in the boat and come back to the administration office, lie down on the floor and nobody could get near him, he wouldn't say a word. And if you said anything to cross him, he'd face the corner and start crying . . . he'd stand there crying and pee on the floor like a kid."

Suddenly Grandad fell silent. His lips became twisted, his blue nose flared up and went out. He cried. Cried like a woman, grabbing his head in his hands, his shoulders trembling and shaking in waves.

"Well, is that all, Mitrich?"

The car shuddered with laughter. Everyone laughed an ugly laugh and a happy laugh. And the grandson even started tugging at himself from top to bottom so as not to wet both ankles. The man with the black moustache got angry:

"So where's Turgenev here? We made a deal: 'Like in Turgenev!' But here the devil knows what's going on. Somebody covered with boils who pees, to boot!"

"Ah, he probably's retelling a moving picture," someone grumbled from the side. "The moving picture *The Chairman*."

And I sat there and understood old Mitrich, understood

his tears—he was simply sorry for everything and everyone, sorry for the chairman because he had been given such a shameful nickname, and for the wall on which he urinated, and for the boat and the boils—sorry for everything. First love or ultimate pity, what's the difference? God, dying on the cross, preached pity to us, and, not scoffing, did he preach. Pity and love for the world are one. Love and pity for every womb, and for the fruit of every womb.

"Go on, Gramp," I said to him. "Go on, I'm treating you, you've earned it. You did a good job on love.

"And all of you, let's drink. To the nobleman from Oryol, Ivan Turgenev, citizen of *la belle France*."

"Let's. To the nobleman from Oryol . . ."

Again the same gurgle and the same sound, then again the rustling and smacking of lips. An encore of the Rhapsody in C sharp minor composed by Franz Liszt.

No one noticed right away that at the door of our coupé (let's call it a coupé) there had appeared the figure of a woman with a black moustache in a brown beret and a jacket. She was completely drunk, inside and out, and her beret had gotten askew.

"I also want to drink to Turgenev," she enunciated from her very guts.

The confusion lasted no more than a couple of moments.

"A tantalizing morsel arrives during the meal," the Decembrist taunted her. Everybody laughed.

"What's to laugh at?" Grandad said. "Just another woman, nice, soft . . ."

"Nice women like that," the man with the black

moustache retorted sadly, "nice women like that should be shipped to the Crimea and fed to the wolves."

"But why, why?" I protested, and started fussing about. "Let her sit down. Let her tell something. You've read Turgenev, you've read Maksim Gorky, but try and get any sense out of you . . ." I sat her down and poured her out a half a glass of "Aunt Clara's."

She drank it and, in place of a thank you, she lifted up the beret from her head: "Look here, do you see that?" And she showed us all a scar above her ear, and then was majestically silent, and then extended her glass toward me once more: "Hit me again, young man, otherwise I'll faint."

I poured her another half a glass.

PAVLOVO-POSAD—NAZARIEVO

She drank that one too, rather mechanically. And having drunk it, she opened her mouth wide and showed everyone: "Do you see, there are four teeth missing?" "So where are they, these teeth?" "Who knows where they are? I'm an educated woman but I'm walking around without teeth. He knocked them out for me because of Pushkin. And when I heard how you're having such a literary conversation here, I thought, Go on and join them, have a drink and at the same time tell how your head was broken and four of your front teeth knocked out because of Pushkin."

So she set about telling her story:

"Everything started with Pushkin. They sent us a Komsomol organizer, Evtushenkin, he was always

97

pinching me and reciting poetry, and once he catches hold of me by the calves and asks: 'Has my wondrous gaze tormented thee?' I say, 'What if it has?' But, by the calves again: 'Has my voice resounded in thy soul?' Then he grabs me in his arms and drags me off somewhere. And when he drags me out again I go around, days, not myself, repeating over and over: 'Pushkin . . . Evtushenkin . . . tormented . . . resounded,' 'Resounded . . . tormented . . . Evtushenkin . . . Pushkin.' And then again: 'Pushkin . . . Evtushenkin . . .' ''

"Get on with it, get on with the front teeth," the man with the black moustache cut her short.

"Right away, right away with the teeth. You'll get your teeth. What next? So from then on everything went OK, a whole half year I called down God's ire with him in the hayloft. And then this Pushkin spoils everything again. I'm just like Joan of Arc—not made for pasturing the cows and sowing wheat—she up and got her butt on a horse and galloped into Orléans to seek adventures. Just like me, I get a little drunk and right away I go up to him: 'And who's going to educate your kids for you? Pushkin, is it?' And he snarls: 'And what kids've we got? There ain't any kids here. What's Pushkin got to do with it?' And then I'd answer: 'When there are some kids, it'll be too late to remember Pushkin.'

"And so, every time, I'd only have to get a little drunk. 'Who'll educate the kids?' I'd say, 'Pushkin is it?' and he'd straight away go crazy. 'Leave, Dariya,' he yells. 'Leave.' Stop chipping away at a man's soul.' I hated him at those times, I hated him so much that I'd get a headache behind my eyes. And, then, no matter, I'd love him again, love him so much that at night I'd wake up from it.

"And then somehow I got stinking drunk. I fly up to him and yell: 'Pushkin will educate your kids for you? Huh? Pushkin?'

"As soon as he hears 'Pushkin' he turns all black and starts to shake: 'Drink, get drunk, but don't mention Pushkin, don't mention kids. Drink everything, drink my blood and don't tempt your Lord God.' And at this time I was out on sick leave, a brain concussion and twisted bowels, and it was fall then in the South, and I started yelling, 'Leave me, murderer, leave for good. I'll get along, I'll sleep around for a month and throw myself under a train and then I'll go to a convent and take the veil. You'll come to beg forgiveness from me and I'll come out all in black, all enchanting, and I'll make a fig and scratch your eyes out with it! Leave!' And then I scream: 'Do you at least love the soul in me? The soul?' And he shakes all over and turns black: 'With my heart,' he yells, 'with my heart, yes, with my heart I love your soul, but, no, I don't love your soul with my soul!!'

"And wild somehow, like in an opera, he burst out laughing and grabbed me and broke my skull and left for Vladimir-on-the-Kliazma. Why did he leave? To whom did he go? All Europe shared my doubts. But a month later he returned. And at that time I was in a drunken fog and as soon as I saw him, I fell down on the table, burst out laughing and started rubbing my legs together: 'Aha,' I started screaming, 'you blew it in Vladimir-on-the-Kliazma, but who'll educate the kids . . .' And he doesn't

99

say a word, he just comes over and knocks out my four front teeth and leaves for Rostov-on-the-Don, on Komsomol business.

"I'm ready to faint, boy. Hit me again, light . . ."

We all died laughing.

"And where is he now, your Evtushenkin?"

"Who knows, where? Either in Siberia or in Central Asia. If he got to Rostov and is still alive, that means he's somewhere in Central Asia. But if he didn't get to Rostov and died, that means he's in Siberia."

"You're right," I backed her up, "you won't die in Central Asia, it's possible to live in Central Asia. I've not been there myself but this friend of mine, Tikhonov, has been.

"He says you go along and see a settlement and they burn dried dung in the stoves, but there's nothing to drink, though there's plenty of victuals: yurts and mullah. That's what he took for nourishment almost a half a year: yurts and mullah. And it's not so bad—he came back all mellow with his eyes bulging."

"And in Siberia?"

"And in Siberia—no, you'll die. In general nobody can live in Siberia, only black people live there. Products are not transported in, there's nothing to drink, not to speak of a 'meal.' Only once a year from Zhitomir, in the Ukraine, embroidered towels are brought in and the blacks hang themselves with them."

"And what sort of blacks?" The Decembrist, who had been on the point of dozing off, bestirred himself. "What blacks are there in Siberia? Blacks live in the States, not in Siberia. You've been to Siberia, I suppose. But have you been to the States?"

100

"I have been. And I didn't see any kind of blacks there."

"No blacks? In the States?"

"Yes, in the States. Not one black."

Everyone had succeeded in getting so numb, and everyone's head was so foggy, that there was no room for any kind of perplexity. The woman with the complicated story and a scar and no teeth was quickly forgotten. And she forgot herself as well, and all the others forgot themselves.

"Which means you've been in the States," the man with the black moustache mumbled. "That's very, very extraordinary. There aren't any blacks there and never were any, that I'll accept . . . I believe you like a brother . . . But, tell us, was there no freedom there either? And freedom thus remains a phantom on that continent of sorrow, as they write in our newspapers? Tell us."

"Yes," I responded, "and freedom thus remains a phantom on that continent of sorrow, and the people, thus, have become so used to it that they almost don't notice. Just think, they don't have—I walked around a lot and observed them closely—not in a single grimace or gesture or remark do they have anything like the awkwardness to which we have become accustomed. On every rotten face there is as much dignity expressed in a minute as would last us for our whole great Seven Year Plan. 'How come?' I thought, and turned off Manhattan onto Fifth Avenue and answered my own question: 'Because of their vile self-satisfaction—nothing else.' But where do they get their self-satisfaction?? I froze in the middle of the Avenue in order to resolve the thought: 'In the world of propagandistic fictions and advertising vagaries, where do they get so much self-satisfaction?' I was heading into Harlem and shrugged my shoulders. 'Where? The playthings of monopoly's ideologues, the marionettes of the arms kings, where do they get such appetite? They gorge five times a day and always with the same endless dignity—but can a man have a real appetite in the States?' "

"Yes, yes, yes," old Mitrich nodded his head. "They eat OK there, but we almost don't eat at all . . . all our rice goes to China, all the sugar to Cuba . . . so what will we eat?"

"Nothing, Pops, nothing . . . You've already eaten yours, it's a sin to talk like that. If you get to the States, remember the main thing: don't forget your Homeland and don't forget its goodness. Maksim Gorky didn't write only about the ladies, he wrote about the Homeland too. You remember what he wrote?"

"What you mean . . . I remember . . ." And everything he had drunk could be seen in his blue eyes. "I remember: 'I went off farther and farther into the woods with grandmother' . . ."

"You mean to say that's about the Homeland, Mitrich?" the man with the black moustache slurred angrily. "That's about grandmother, not the Homeland at all!"

And Mitrich started crying again.

NAZARIEVO—DREZNA

And the man with the black moustache said, "Here you've seen a lot and traveled a lot. Tell us, where do they value the Russian more, on this or the other side of the Pyrenees?"

"I don't know about this side. But on the other they don't value him at all. For example, I was in Italy. There, there's no attention paid to the Russian. They only sing and draw there. One of them, let's say, gets up and sings. And another, sitting alongside, draws the first one who's singing. And a third, sitting off to the side, sings about the one who's drawing. And they don't understand our grief."

"Ah, the Italians, do they really understand anything?" the man with the black moustache backed me up.

"Precisely. When I was in Italy, on St. Mark's day, I wanted to take a look at the boat races. And how sad they made me. My heart dissolved in tears, though my lips were silent. But the Italians didn't understand, they laughed and pointed their fingers at me. 'Hey, look, Erofeev is going around fucked up again.' But really was I so fucked up? My lips simply were silent.

"Actually there was no reason for me to be in Italy. I only wanted to see three things: Vesuvius, Herculaneum, and Pompeii. But they said that Vesuvius disappeared long ago and sent me to Herculaneum. But in Herculaneum they said, 'So, what do you need with Herculaneum, you idiot? It'd be better to go to Pompeii.' I arrive in Pompeii but they say to me, 'You've had it with Pompeii. Be off to Herculaneum.'

"With a wave of my hand, I set out for France. I go along and get up to the Maginot Line and suddenly I decide to return and spend some time at Luigi Longo's, I'll rent a cot from him and read books and stop fiddling around. Better to rent a cot from Palmiro Togliatti, of course, but he died recently, you know. But in what way is Luigi Longo worse?

"But I didn't return after all. I went instead across the

Tyrol in the direction of the Sorbonne. I arrive at the Sorbonne and I say, 'I want to study for my bachelor's.' But they tell me, 'If you want to study for your bachelor's, buddy, you have to have something like an inherent phenomenon in you. So what kind of inherent phenomenon do you have in you?' What could I say? I say, 'Well, what kind of inherent phenomenon could I have? I'm just a kid, you know.' 'From Siberia?' they ask. 'From Siberia!' 'Well, since you're from Siberia there could be something inherent about your psychology. So what's inherent about your psychology?' I thought about it— after all, this isn't Podunksk, it's the Sorbonne, you've got to say something intelligent. I thought about it and said, 'The inherent phenomenon in me is my self-motivated logos.' But the Rector of the Sorbonne, while I was thinking of something intelligent, had sneaked around behind me and—whack—in the back of the neck; 'You're a fool, Erofeev, and no kind of logos. Get!' he screams. 'Get out of our Sorbonne, Erofeev.' Then for the first time I was sorry that I hadn't rented a cot from Luigi Longo.

''What was left for me to do but go to Paris? I arrive. I head for Notre Dame, I'm going along, and I'm amazed: there's nothing but brothels on every side. Only the Eiffel Tower stands there and General de Gaulle is up on it eating chestnuts and looking in all four directions through binoculars. But what's the sense of looking in all four directions if there's nothing but brothels?

''It's impossible to walk along a boulevard there. Everybody is scurrying from brothel to clinic, from clinic and back to brothel. And there's so much gonorrhea around that it's difficult to walk on the Champs-Élysées, there's so much gonorrhea around I can hardly move my feet. I see a couple of acquaintances, he and she, they're both chewing on chestnuts, and both old. Where did I see them? In the newspapers? I don't remember. Presently I recognized them: that was Louis Aragon and Elsa Triole. 'It's interesting,' the thought slips through my head. 'From clinic to brothel or from brothel to clinic?' And I cut myself off, 'You should be ashamed. You're in Paris, not Podunksk. Ask them questions of social significance, the most agonizing social questions.'

"I catch up to Louis Aragon and open up my heart and say that I despair of everything, that I have no doubts about anything, that I am dying from internal contradictions, and much more in that vein, but he only looked at me, saluted like an old veteran, took his Elsa by the arm and walked off. I catch up again and this time talk not to Louis but to Triole: I say that I'm dying from a lack of impressions and that I'm overcome by doubts just when I stop despairing, while in moments of despair I don't know any doubts . . . but like an old whore she patted me on the cheek, took her Aragon by the arm, and walked off.

"Later, of course, I learned from the papers that they weren't Louis and Elsa at all; it turns out they were Jean-Paul Sartre and Simone de Beauvoir, but what's the difference to me now? I went about Notre Dame and rented a mansard room there. Mansard, mezzanine, wing, entresol and attic—I'm always getting them mixed up and don't see any difference. Briefly, I rented that in which it is possible to lie down, to write, and to smoke a pipe. I smoked up twelve pipes and sent off to the Revue de Paris my essay on questions of love.

"And you know yourselves how hard it is to write about love in France. Because, in France, everything concerned with love has long since been written. There, everybody knows everything, while we don't know anything about love. Show our citizen with average education a crab louse and ask him if it's an ordinary one or a crab louse, and he'll blurt out, 'An ordinary one, of course.' But show him an ordinary one and he loses his head entirely. But in France, no. There, they may not know how much a bottle of Trapper's costs, but if it's an ordinary louse then it'll be ordinary to everyone and nobody will call it a crab.

"In other words, the Revue de Paris returned my essay with the excuse that it was written in Russian, that only the title was in French. Do you think that I fell into despair? I smoked thirteen more pipes in my entresol and created a new essay also dedicated to love. This time it was written in French from beginning to end. Only the title was Russian (and after Ilich at that): Bitchiness as the Highest and Final Stage of Whoredom. And sent it off to the Revue de Paris."

"And they returned it to you again?" the man with the black moustache asked, to indicate that he was participating in the conversation, but as if in his sleep.

"It goes without saying, they returned it. They recognized my language as brilliant but the basic idea as false. 'It may be applicable to Russian conditions,' they said, 'but not to the French. Bitchiness here,' they said, 'is not yet the highest stage and certainly not the ultimate one. With you, with you Russians, your whoredom, having reached the limit of bitchiness, will be forcibly abolished and replaced by onanism in an obligatory program; with us, with us French, although not excluded in the future, there is an inculcation (in a more voluntary program) of certain elements of Russian onanism, in a native Sodom into which our bitchiness, through incest, is being transformed. But this inculcation will proceed in the course of traditional whoredom and in quite a permanent condition.'

"Briefly, they crapped on my brains completely. So that I spat on it, burned my manuscripts together with the mansard and the entresol, and took off for the English Channel through Verdun. Along toward Albion, I went along thinking, 'All the same, why didn't I stay in Luigi Longo's apartment?' I walked along and sang, 'The Queen of England is seriously ill, if she lives till tomorrow she'll be here still!' But in the outskirts of London . . .''

"Permit me,'' the man with the black moustache interrupted. "Your boldness astonishes me . . . no, I believe you like a brother . . . the ease with which you overcame all national boundaries astonishes me.''

DREZNA—KILOMETER 85

"So what's so astonishing about it? And what boundaries, anyway? A boundary is necessary in order not to get nations confused. With us, for example, a border guard stands there and he knows absolutely that the boundary isn't a fiction or an emblem, because on one side of it people speak Russian and drink more and on the other they speak non-Russian and drink less.

"But over there what kind of boundaries could exist, if they all drink and speak non-Russian in the same way?

Over there, they might like to set out a border guard, but there'd be no place to set him. So over there the border guards hang around without anything to do, grieving and bumming cigarettes. In this sense, things are completely free. If you want, for example, to stay in Eboli, please, stay in Eboli. If you want to go to Canosa, nobody'll interfere with you, go to Canosa. If you want to cross the Rubicon, go ahead.

"So there's nothing astonishing about it . . . At twelve-zero-zero Greenwich time I had already been introduced to the Director of the British Museum, whose euphonious and idiotic name was something like Sir Silage Corn. 'What do you want from us?' the Director of the British Museum asked. 'I want to become *engagé* here. More likely, I want you to *engager* me, that's what I want.'

" 'You want me to *engager* you in those pants?' said the Director of the British Museum. 'What about these pants?' I asked him with concealed vexation. And he, as if he hadn't heard, got in front of me on all fours and started smelling my socks. Having smelled them, he got up, frowned, spat, and then asked: 'In those socks, you want me to *engager* you?'

" 'What about these socks?' I started to say, not concealing my vexation anymore. 'What about them? Take the socks I dragged around in my Homeland; they really smelled, yes. But before departure I changed them, because everything in man ought to be beautiful—his soul and his thoughts and his . . .'

"But he didn't even want to listen. Went into the Chamber of Lords and said to them, 'Lords, I've got a bum here behind the door. He's from snow-covered Russia but, it would seem, not terribly drunk. What am I to do with this miserable wretch, *engager* him, the scarecrow, or not give the straw man any *engagement* at all?' And the Lords looked me over through their monocles and said, 'Give it a try, Si, give it a try. Put him up for review. This dusty bastard would fit in in any interior.' Here, the Queen of England took the floor. She raised her hand and cried . . .''

"Watch it, Ticket Control!" The cry rang out, exploding through the length of the train. "Ticket Control!"

My story was interrupted in the most interesting of places. But not only was my story interrupted: the drunken half-daze that the man with the black moustache was in, the Decembrist's sleep—everything was interrupted in midstream. Old Mitrich came to, all in tears. Only the woman of the complicated story, who had covered her missing teeth with her beret, slept, like a *Fata Morgana*.

Strictly speaking, on the Petushki branch line no one was afraid of ticket inspectors, since no one ever had a ticket. If some crazy boozer or other broke the rule and bought a ticket, he would, of course, feel uncomfortable when the inspectors appeared. He would stare down at his feet as if he wanted to sink into the ground. And the inspector would look at the ticket squeamishly and give the man a withering glance as if he were some sort of garbage. While the people would look with big, beautiful eyes at this character, as if to say, "Look at the ground, you shitass, your conscience has gotten the better of you." And they'd look the inspector in the eye with even more determination: "Take a look at us. Can you judge us? Come on over here, Semenych, we won't offend you."

Before Semenych had become the chief inspector, things were very different. In those days, riders without tickets were chased onto the reservation like Hindus, flogged over the head with the Academy Dictionary and then fined and kicked off the train. In those days, people would race through the cars in droves to dodge an inspector, dragging along even those with tickets. Once, two small boys were caught up in the general panic, ran off with the herd, and were crushed to death before my eyes. They lay as they fell between cars; their little hands, turning blue, still clutched their tickets.

Chief Inspector Semenych changed all that. He cancelled all the fines and the drives to the reservation. He made things simpler; he accepted one gram of vodka per kilometer from anyone without a ticket. All over Russia drivers take a kopek per kilometer from hitchhikers, but Semenych was one and a half times cheaper—one gram per kilometer. If, for instance, you're going from Chukhlinki to Usad—a distance of ninety kilometers—you pour out ninety grams for Semenych and off you go sprawled on your bench like a fat cat.

Thus Semenych's innovation strengthened the bond between the inspector and the broad masses; he made this bond cheaper, simpler, and more humane. And now at the cry, "Ticket Control," there is no real fear, only anticipation.

Semenych came into the car, smiling carnivorously. He was already hardly able to stand up. Usually, he rode only to Orekhovo-Zuevo, where he would jump off and go into his office, having collected enough to get puking drunk.

"Is that you, Mitrich? Going to Orekhovo with your grandson again to ride the merry-go-round? That'll be 180 for the two of you. Is that you, black moustache? Salty-kovskaya to Orekhovo-Zuevo? Seventy-two grams. Wake up that whore and ask how much is due from her. And you, Worsted Coat, from where to where? Hammer & Sickle to Pokrov? One hundred and five, be so kind. It's getting so you can't find anyone with a ticket anymore. Once this called for 'public anger and outrage' but now it's just 'justified pride.' And you, Venya?"

And Semenych bathed me with a bloodthirsty whiff of his alcoholic breath.

"And you, Venya? Moscow—Petushki, to the end of the line as usual?"

KILOMETER 85—OREKHOVO-ZUEVO

"Yes, as usual. And it's for good this time: Moscow—Petushki . . ."

"And you think you'll worm your way out of it this time, Scheherazade? Right?"

Here I must make a small digression and, while Semenych is drinking the dosage that he's collected in fines, explain to you quickly why "Scheherazade" and what he meant by "worm your way out of it."

Three years have passed since I first bumped into Semenych. Then, he had only just started to work as an inspector. He came up to me and said, "Moscow—Petushki? One hundred twenty-five." And, when I didn't understand what was what, he explained it to me. And, when I said that I didn't have a drop with me, his answer to that was: "Do I have to kick your ass around for you, if

111

you haven't got any?" I answered him that it wouldn't be necessary and muttered something from the area of Roman law. He became terribly interested and asked me to tell him in detail about everything ancient and Roman. I started to talk and soon got to the scandalous tale of Lucretia and Tarquinius, but, at this point, he had to jump off at Orekhovo-Zuevo. So he didn't get a chance to find out what finally happened to Lucretia: did that good-for-nothing Tarquinius attain his end or not . . .

Now Semenych was an extraordinary ladies' man and a utopian; the history of the world interested him only for its intimate moments. So when he looked in again a week later near Friazevo, Semenych didn't say to me, "Moscow—Petushki? One hundred twenty-five." No, he flung himself on me for the continuation: "Well, did he fuck his Lucretia or not?"

And I told him what happened next. I went from Roman to Christian history and came to the story of Hypatia.

"And so, at the instigation of the Patriarch Cyril, the monks of Alexandria, seized by fanaticism, tore the clothing from the beautiful Hypatia and . . ." But, here, our train came to a dead stop in Orekhovo-Zuevo, and Semenych had to leap onto the platform, hopelessly intrigued.

And in this way three years passed, every week. On the Moscow—Petushki line I was the only unticketed passenger who had never brought Semenych a single gram of vodka and, nevertheless, remained unabused and among the living. But every story has an end—even the story of the world.

The next Friday, I got up to Indira Gandhi, Moshe Dayan, and Dubček. There was no place left to go.

And so Semenych drank the fines he had levied, grunted and looked at me like a boa constrictor.

"Moscow—Petushki? One hundred twenty-five."

"Semenych," I responded, almost begging, "Semenych, haven't you drunk quite a lot already?"

"A decent amount," he answered, not without self-satisfaction. He was really foggy.

"Then that means you've got an imagination? That means you're ready to race into the future? That means you can come with me out of the dark world of the past into the golden age which 'verily, verily, shall be'!"

"I can, Venya, I can. Today, I can do anything."

"From the Third Reich, the Fifth Republic, from Slaughterhouse Five, the Seventeenth Congress—can you leap with me into the promised land of the Fifth Kingdom, the seventh heaven and the Second Coming?"

"I can," Semenych roared. "Speak, Scheherazade, speak!"

"Then, listen. The day will come, that day of days. On that day when most weary Simon shall say finally, 'Now, absolve thy servant, Lord,' and the archangel Gabriel shall say, 'Hail, Mary, blessed art thou amongst women,' and Doctor Faust shall pronounce: 'The moment is now, linger and stop a bit!' And all whose names are written in the book of life shall sing out: 'Exalt Isaiah,' and Diogenes will extinguish his lantern. There shall be good and beauty and everything will be fine and all will be good and other than good and beauty there will be nothing and all shall merge into a kiss."

"Merge into a kiss." Semenych was fidgeting impatiently now.

"Yes! And the torturer and the victim shall merge into a

kiss, and spite, design, and calculation shall disappear from the heart, and the woman—"

"The woman!!" Semenych started to quiver. "What? What about the woman?"

"And the woman of the East shall throw off her veil, the oppressed woman of the East shall throw off her veil once and for all, and the lamb shall lie down."

"Lie down?" Here he started to twitch all over.

"Yes. And the lamb shall lie down with the wolf and not one tear shall be shed and every cavalier shall choose a lady, whoever pleases him, and . . ."

"Ooooh," Semenych groaned. "Will she? Will it be soon?" And, suddenly, he started to wave his hands like a gypsy dancer and then to fumble busily about with his clothing, stripping off his uniform down to his most intimate parts.

Although drunk, I gazed at him in amazement, while the sober citizens around him just about leapt from their seats. And in dozens of eyes was written a huge "Aha!" The people had interpreted the matter quite differently than they ought to have interpreted it.

I should tell you that homosexuality in our country has been overcome once and for all but not entirely. Or, entirely but not completely. Or else, entirely and completely but not once and for all. What do people think about now? Nothing but homosexuality. That and the Middle East. Israel, the Golan Heights, Moshe Dayan. So, if they chase Moshe Dayan off the Golan Heights and the Arabs make peace with the Jews? What will remain in the peoples' heads? Nothing but homosexuality pure and simple.

Let's say they're watching television: General de Gaulle and Georges Pompidou meet at a diplomatic function. Naturally they both smile and shake each other's hand. And then the audience goes: "Aha." They say, "Go on, General de Gaulle!" Or: "Aha, go on, Georges Pompidou!"

Just like they were looking at us now. Everyone had "Aha" written in his round eyes.

"Semenych! Semenych!" I grabbed him under the arms and started to drag him toward the vestibule. "People are looking at us. Come to your senses . . . Let's go!"

He was terribly heavy. He had gotten all soft and unsteady. I barely got him to the end of the car and propped up against the automatic doors.

"Venya, tell me . . . the woman of the East . . . If she takes off the veil . . . will she have anything else on? Does she have anything under the veil?"

I had no time to answer. The train stopped as if transfixed at the station in Orekhovo-Zuevo, and the doors opened automatically.

OREKHOVO-ZUEVO

Senior Inspector Semenych, intrigued for the one thousand and first time, half-alive and unbuttoned, was propelled out onto the platform, bumping his head on the railing. He then collapsed under the feet of the people getting off the train, and all the fines he had collected spewed out of his gullet and flowed away over the platform.

I saw all of this with complete clarity, and report on it to the world. But all the rest I didn't see and cannot report on. At the very edge of my consciousness, I was aware that the human avalanche which was getting off at Orekhovo overwhelmed me and sucked at me so as to gather me into itself like a nasty wad to be spit out on the Orekhovo platform. But without quite spitting, because the people getting on the train plugged up the mouth of the ones getting off.

And if God should ask me: "Really, Venya, you don't remember anything else? Really, did you immediately sink into that sleep with which all your calamities began?" I'll say to him, "No, Lord, not immediately. At the very same edge of consciousness, I was also aware that I was able, finally, to get the better of the elements and to break through into the empty spaces of the train and to fall onto somebody's bench, the one next to the door.

"And when I had fallen onto the bench, Lord, I immediately gave myself over to the potent flow of dreams and lazy somnolence—oh, no. I'm lying again, I'm again lying to thy face, Lord. It is not I who lie, it's my weakened memory. I did not immediately give myself over to the flow, I groped in my pocket for the still-sealed bottle of Kubanskaya and took five or six sips—and only then, shipping the oars, did I give myself over to the potent flow of dreams and lazy somnolence.

"All your fancies about the Golden Age," I repeated over and over, "all are lies and dejection. But me, twelve weeks ago, I saw its prototype and a half hour from now its reflection will flash in my eyes for the thirteenth time. There, the birds never cease singing neither by day nor by night; there, neither winter nor summer does the jasmine cease blooming, but what's that in the jasmine? Who is it there, arrayed in purple and linen, with the downcast eyes, smelling the lilies?"

And I smile like an idiot and pull aside the branches of jasmine.

OREKHOVO-ZUEVO—KRUTOE

And a sleepy Tikhonov emerges from the branches of jasmine, squinting into the sun.

"What are you doing here, Tikhonov?"

"I'm finishing work on the theses. Everything has long been ready except for the theses. And now, here, the theses are ready too."

"Does this mean that you consider that the time is ripe?"

"Who knows? The moment I have a little something to drink, it seems to me that it is, but the minute I start coming down—no, I think, it's not yet ripe and it is still too soon to take up arms."

"Better drink some Hollands, Vadya."

Tikhonov drank some Hollands, grunted, and fell to grieving.

"Well, what? Is the time ripe?"

"Wait a minute, it's getting there."

"When do we act? Tomorrow?"

"Who knows! The moment I have a little something to drink it seems to me that even today—that even yesterday—wasn't too early to act. But the minute I start coming down, no, I think that yesterday was too early and that the day after tomorrow won't be too late."

117

"Better drink some more Hollands, Vadimchik, drink some more Hollands."

Vadimchik took a drink and again fell to grieving.

"Well, what? Do you think it's time?"

"It is."

"Don't forget the password. And tell everyone not to forget: tomorrow morning halfway between the villages of Garino and Eliseikovo, by the cattle yard, at nine-zero-zero Greenwich . . ."

"Right. Nine-zero-zero Greenwich."

"Goodbye, comrade. Try to get some sleep on this night."

"I'll try to get some sleep. Goodbye, comrade."

Here I must qualify: in the face of the conscience of the whole of mankind I should say that from the very beginning I opposed this adventure, fruitless as a fig tree. (Well said, "Fruitless as a fig tree"!) From the very first, I said that revolution achieves something essential when it occurs in the heart and not in the town square. But once they began it without me, I could not remain aloof from those who began it. I would be able, in any case, to avert unnecessary bitterness of heart and to lessen the amount of bloodshed.

Before nine Greenwich, in the grass next to the cattle yard, we sat and waited. To everyone who came up, we said, "Sit down with us; take a load off your feet, comrade," and they all remained standing, clanked their weapons and repeated the agreed-upon phrase from Pushkin's *Eugene Onegin:* "I love the ladies' dainty feet." This password was playful and ambiguous, but we weren't up to that—nine-zero-zero Greenwich was approaching.

With what did it all begin? It all began with Tikhonov nailing his fourteen theses to the gate of the Eliseikovo Agro-Soviet. Rather he didn't nail them to the gate but wrote them on the fence with chalk and they were more like words and not theses, clear and lapidary words, and there were only two of them and not fourteen, but, be that as it may, it all began with that.

We moved out in two columns with our standards in our hands. One column marched on Eliseikovo, the other on Tartino. And we marched without opposition till sunset. No one was killed on any side, no one was wounded either, only one prisoner was taken—the elderly ex-Chairman of the Larionovo Agro-Soviet, removed from his post for drunkenness and congenital imbecility. Eliseikovo was subdued. Cherkasovo lay prostrate at our feet; Neugodovo and Peksha begged for mercy. All the population centers of the Petushki district from the store at Poloshy to the Andreevo village storehouse—all were occupied by the forces of the rebellion.

And after sunset, the village of Cherkasovo was proclaimed the capital, the prisoner was brought there, and there, too, a congress of the victors was improvised. Everyone who delivered a speech was stinking drunk; they all ground on about one and the same thing: Maximilian, Robespierre, Oliver Cromwell, Sonya Perovskaya, Vera Zasulich, punitive detachments from Petushki, war with Norway and, again, Sonya Perovskaya, Vera Zasulich . . .

Some listeners cried, "And Norway, where is that anyway?" "Who knows anyhow, where it is!" Others answered them, "Halfway to hell and back." "Wherever it is," I tried to calm them down, "we won't get anywhere without intervention. In order to restore the economy destroyed by war, we must first destroy it, and for that you need a civil war, at least some kind of a war . . . you need a minimum of twelve fronts."

"White Polish forces are needed," Tikhonov cried, staggering drunk. "Oh, idiot," I interrupted him, "you're always running off at the mouth. You're a brilliant theoretician, Vadim; we have nailed your theses to our hearts, but as soon as the time comes, you're pure shit, you fool, what do you need with White Polish forces?" "So, am I arguing?" Tikhonov started giving in. "As if they're more necessary to me than to you! Norway's OK with me."

In the heat of the moment everyone somehow had forgotten that Norway had been a member of NATO for twenty years, and Vladik Ts—sky was already running to the Larionovo post office with a package of cards and letters. One letter was addressed, return receipt, to Olaf, King of Norway, declaring war. Another letter—rather not even a letter but a blank piece of paper sealed in an envelope—was sent off to General Franco. Let him see an accusatory finger in that, the old dolt, let him turn pale as the piece of paper, the fucking Caudillo. From the Prime Minister of Great Britain, Harold Wilson, we demanded very little: "Get your gunboat out of the Gulf of Aqaba, Prime Minister, then do as you wish. . . ." And finally, in a fourth letter to Wladyslaw Gomulka, we wrote: "You, Wladyslaw, have full and inalienable right to the Polish corridor, while Józef Cyrankievicz hasn't the slightest claim to the Polish Corridor. . . ."

And we sent four postcards: to Abba Eban, Moshe

Dayan, General Suharto, and Alexander Dubček. All four postcards were quite lovely, with little scenes and acorn designs. So let the boys enjoy them, the louts; maybe they'll recognize us as subjects of international law.

No one slept that night. Everyone was seized by enthusiasm, everyone gazed at the sky waiting for Norwegian bombs, the opening of the stores, and intervention. And everyone imagined how happy Wladyslaw Gomulka would be and how Józef Cyrankievicz would tear his hair.

The prisoner didn't sleep either; the ex-Chairman of the Agro-Soviet howled from his shed like a grieving hound.

"Boys! . . . Does this mean that tomorrow morning nobody'll bring me anything to drink?"

"Hey, whadaya want! Give thanks that at least we'll feed you in accordance with the Geneva Convention."

"What's that, anyway?"

"You'll see what it is. That is, you'll still be able to drag your feet about, Ivanych, but you won't be much for sniffing around the ladies."

KRUTOE—VOINOVO

And a Plenum was in season from dawn until the time the liquor stores opened up. It was broad-based and revolutionary-spirited, but since all four of our Plenums were broad-based and revolutionary-spirited, we decided, in order not to get them mixed up, to number them: First Plenum, Second Plenum, Third Plenum, and Fourth Plenum.

The entire First Plenum was devoted to electing a

President, i.e., to electing me as President. This took us some two minutes, no more. So all the rest of the time was eaten up by debate on a purely speculative theme: Who'll open up the store earlier—Aunty Masha in Andreevo or Aunty Shura in Polomy?

Sitting on my presidium, I listened to the debate and thought, debate is absolutely necessary—but decrees are much more necessary. Why are we forgetting that which should be the crowning labor of any revolution—the issuing of decrees? For example, a decree obligating Aunty Shura in Polomy to open her store at six in the morning. Nothing could be simpler: invested with the power, we undertake to force Aunty Shura to open her store at six in the morning instead of nine-thirty. Why didn't this occur to me before?

Or, for example, a decree concerning land: transferring to the people all the land in the district, all acreage and all movable property, along with all alcoholic beverages and without any requital? Or this: resetting the hands of the clock two hours forward or an hour and a half back, or any way whatever. Then demanding that the word "devil" be spelled with a capital D, or cancelling some letter altogether—it's just a question of which one. And, finally, forcing Aunty Masha in Andreevo to open her store at five-thirty instead of nine.

Thoughts crowded into my head, so much so that I started to feel sad and called Tikhonov off behind the scenes, where we drank some Caraway vodka and I said:

"Hey listen, counselor!"

"Well, what?"

"Oh, nothing. You're a shitty counselor, that's what."

"Find another one." Tikhonov was offended.

"That's not the point, Vadya. The point is this: if you're a decent counselor, sit down and write decrees. Have another little drink, sit down and write. I heard that you have not restrained yourself after all, that you pinched Anatole Ivanych's thigh. What are you up to? You want to start a terror campaign?"

"Oh, what the . . . Just a little . . ."

"And what sort of terror are you undertaking? White terror?"

"Yes."

"It's in vain, Vadya. However, OK, right now's not the time. It is necessary to write a decree first, if only one stinking decree. You have paper and pen? Sit down and write. And then we'll have a drink and go on to a declaration of human rights. And only then comes the terror. And then later we'll have a drink and, as Ilich put it, study, study, study."

Tikhonov wrote two words, had a drink, and sighed:

"Yes-s-s . . . I muffed it with my terror . . . Well, really, in our affair it's impossible not to make mistakes, because our affair is unheard-of and new, and consider that there are no precedents. There were precedents, it's true, but . . ."

"Aw, what kind of precedents are they? They're nothing. Nonsense. The flight of the bumblebee, the amusement of spoiled grown-ups—not any kind of precedents. . . . The calendar—what do you think? Should we replace it or leave it as it is?"

"Oh, better leave it. As they say: don't poke around in shit or you'll start smelling."

"You put it correctly, we'll leave it as is. In you I have a brilliant theoretician, Vadya, and that's good. Should we close the Plenum or not? Aunty Shura in Polomy is already open. She has some Rossiiskaya, they say."

"Close it, of course. Anyway, tomorrow morning the Second Plenum will take place. Let's go to Polomy."

Aunty Shura in Polomy really did have some Rossiiskaya. In connection with this, as well as in expectation of punitive raids from the Regional Center, it was decided to move the capital temporarily from Cherkasovo to Polomy—that is, twelve versts deeper into the territory of the Republic.

And there, on the next morning, the Second Plenum, devoted to the issue of my resignation from the Presidency, was declared open.

"I am getting up from the President's chair," I said. "I spit in the President's chair. I feel that the President's chair should be occupied by someone who looks so shot from drink that you couldn't touch his face with a three-day beating. Do we actually have anyone like that?" "We don't," the delegates answered in unison. "Take me, for example, couldn't you touch mine with a three-day beating?"

Everyone looked at me a couple of seconds and then answered in unison: "We could."

"So there you are," I continued. "We'll get along without a President. We'd better do this: let's everybody go into the meadows and make some home-brew, and lock Borya up. Since he's a person of high moral qualities, let him sit there and set up the office."

My speech was interrupted by an ovation, and the Plenum was closed down. The neighboring meadows lit up with the blue fire of the stills. I alone did not share the general animation and optimism. I moved from fire to fire with a single alarming thought: why wasn't anyone in the world willing to have anything to do with us? Why such silence in the world? The district is in flames, and the world is silent because it is holding its breath, perhaps, but why has no one extended his hand—not from the east, not from the west? What's become of King Olaf? Why don't regular units crush us from the south?

Quietly I led the counselor to the side—he reeked of home-brew.

"Do you like our revolution, Vadya?"

"Yes," Vadya answered. "It is feverish but it is beautiful."

"So . . . But about Norway, Vadya, about Norway, what's new?"

"Nothing so far . . . But what do you care about Norway?

"What do you mean, what do I care? Are we in a state of war with Norway or are we not in a state? Everything is turning out pretty stupid. We're fighting with her, but she doesn't want to with us. If they don't start bombing us by tomorrow, I'll sit down again in the President's chair and then you'll see what'll happen!"

"Sit," Vadya answered. "Who's stopping you, Erofeevkins?" If you want to, go ahead. . . ."

VOINOVO—USAD

Not a single bomb fell on us in the morning. In opening the Third Plenum, I said:

"Senators. I see that no one in the world wants to

125

undertake either to be friends or to quarrel with us. All have turned away from us and have held their breath. And since, tomorrow, punitive detachments from Petushki will arrive here toward evening, and Aunty Shura will be out of Rossiiskaya tomorrow morning, I am taking full power into my hands, and I'm imposing a curfew. And if that's not enough, I declare the powers of the President absolute and at the same time take up the Presidency. That is, become the ''personality above the law and the prophets.''

No one objected. Only Prime Minister Borya S. winced at the word ''prophets,'' looked at me wildly, and started to tremble for vengeance.

Two days later he expired in the arms of the Minister of Defense. He died from grief and from an extreme proclivity for generalization. There didn't seem to be any other causes, but, as to opening him up, we didn't, because to open him up would have been disgusting. And toward evening of the same day, all the world's teletypes received a communication: ''Death was a result of natural causes.'' It wasn't said whose death, but the world surmised.

The Fourth Plenum was a memorial meeting.

I gave a speech:

''Delegates. If I should ever have any children, I'll hang on their wall a portrait of the Procurator of Judaea, Pontius Pilate, so that they will grow up neat and clean. Procurator Pontius Pilate standing there washing his hands—that's the right kind of portrait. Such am I also: I stand here and wash my hands. I joined you simply because I was dead drunk. I told you that it is necessary to revolutionize the heart, that it is necessary to raise souls to the mastery of eternal moral categories, and that everything else that you have undertaken, all that is vanity and chasing of the wind.

"And think, what can we count on? Nobody is going to let us into the Common Market. The ships of America's Seventh Fleet will never make it here, and, really, they won't want to . . ."

At this point they were roaring from their places:

"Don't you despair, Venya! Don't pee in your pants! They'll give us bombardiers! They'll give us B-52's."

"Oh, sure! Hold out your hands! It's indeed funny to listen to you, Senators."

"They'll give us Phantoms, too!"

"Ha, ha. Who said that? 'Phantoms'? One more word about Phantoms and I'll die laughing."

Here, Tikhonov said, from his place:

"Maybe they won't give us Phantoms, but they'll give us devaluation of the franc for sure."

"You're an idiot, Tikhonov, as I see it. I won't argue that you're a valuable theoretician, but every time you open your yap . . . And besides, that's not the point. Why is the whole Petushki region engulfed in flames, but no one, no one takes note of it, not even in the Petushki region? To put it bluntly, I shrug my shoulders and leave my post of President. Like Pontius Pilate I'll wash my hands and, before your eyes, drink up all the rest of the Rossiiskaya. Yes. I trample on my authority—I leave you. For Petushki."

You can imagine what a storm was raised among the delegates, especially when I started to drink up the rest.

And when I started to leave—when I left—you can

imagine what words flew after me. You can also imagine that I will not be repeating these words to you.

There was no repentance in my heart. I went through meadowland and pastures, through sweetbrier thickets and herds of cattle; the grain bowed before me and cornflowers smiled. But, I repeat, there was no repentance in my heart. The sun had set but I went on.

"Heavenly Queen, how far is it still to Petushki?" I said to myself. "I walk and walk and it's nowhere. It's really dark all around—where is Petushki?"

"Where is Petushki, anyhow?" I asked, going up to somebody's lighted veranda. Maybe it wasn't a veranda at all but a terrace, a mezzanine, or a wing? I don't really understand the difference and forever get them mixed up.

I knocked and asked, "Where's Petushki, anyhow? Is it still far to Petushki?" And, in response, everyone on the veranda burst out laughing and didn't say anything. I got offended and knocked again—the neighing on the veranda started up again. Strange. If that wasn't enough, someone was neighing behind my back.

I looked around; the passengers on the Moscow—Petushki train were sitting in their places with filthy smiles on their faces. What's this? So, I'm still on the train?

"It's nothing, Erofeev, nothing. Let them laugh, don't pay any attention. As Saadi said, 'Be straight and simple as a cypress, and generous as a palm.' I don't understand how come the palm, but, OK, be like a palm. Got any Kubanskaya left in your pocket? Yes, I do. There you are—go out to the vestibule and have a drink. Have a drink so you don't get sick."

I got up, hemmed in by a host of idiotic smirks. Alarm welled up from the very dregs of my soul and it was impossible to know what this alarm was all about, where it came from, and why it was so indistinct.

"Are we getting into Usad?" People were crowding around the door expectantly and I turned to them with my question. "Are we getting into Usad?"

"You ask stupid boozy questions when you ought to stay home," some old-timer answered. "You'd better stay home and do tomorrow's lessons. Probably you haven't done tomorrow's stuff yet; your mama'll get mad."

And then he added:

"Hardly out of diapers and he's already learned to think."

What's with him, has he gone off his rocker, this grandad? What mama? What lessons? What pants? Ah no, probably it's not grandad but me who's gone off his rocker. Because this other old-timer with a white, white face stood next to me, looked me in the eye from top to bottom and said:

"Right, and anyway, where do you have to go to? It's too late for you to get betrothed and too early for the cemetery. Where do you have to go to, sweet vagabond?"

"Sweet vagabond!"

I shuddered and went to the other side of the vestibule. Something is amiss in the world. Some kind of rot in the whole kingdom and everybody's got his brains on crooked. Just in case, I felt myself all over . . . what sort of 'sweet vagabond' was I? Where did he get that? What's he been doing, reading Platonov? Sure, you can make a little joke, but nothing quite so nonsensical.

I am in my right mind and they are not, or the other way around: they are all in their right minds, and I alone am not. The feeling of alarm at the bottom of my soul had continued rising. And as we were approaching another stop and the doors started to open, I couldn't resist, and again asked one of the passengers getting off:

"This is Usad, right?"

And (quite unexpectedly) he snapped to attention in front of me and bellowed:

"No, sir!" And then he shook my hand, leaned over, and said in my ear:

"I will never forget your kindness, Comrade First Lieutenant . . ."

And he got off the train, wiping away a tear with his sleeve.

USAD—KILOMETER 105

I remained where I was, in complete loneliness and complete bewilderment. No, not quite bewilderment, but the same alarm turning into bitterness. Then, too, the hell with it—let it be "sweet vagabond" and "First Lieutenant," but why is it dark outside, tell me, please? Why is it dark outside if the train left in the morning and has gone exactly one hundred kilometers? Why?

I leaned my head on the glass . . . what blackness and, beyond the blackness—is that rain or snow? Or is it just that I'm looking through tears into the dark? Oh, God.

"Oh, that's you," someone said from behind my back, in such a pleasant and malicious voice that I didn't even need to turn around. I understood at once who was standing there behind me. "He'll try to tempt me now, the stoneface. He's been waiting for the right time to tempt me!"

"Is that you, Erofeev?" Satan asked.

"Of course it's me, who else?"

"Tough on you, Erofeev, is it?"

"Of course it's tough. Only that doesn't concern you. Get moving, you've got the wrong person."

I continued to speak the same way, with my forehead buried in the window, without turning around.

"Well, if it's tough," Satan went on, "subdue your transport. Subdue your spiritual transport and it'll be easier."

"I won't subdue it for anything."

"What a fool."

"Takes one to know one."

"Well, OK, OK. Then don't say a word. You know what? Better jump out of this moving train. You just might not even get hurt."

I thought about it and then answered, "No-o-o, I won't jump, I'm afraid. I'd have to get hurt."

And Satan left in disgrace.

But what was left for me? I took half a dozen swallows from the bottle and again leaned my head on the window. The blackness went on swimming past the window and stirring up alarm within. And it awakened a black thought. I squeezed my head in order to focus this thought, yet it wouldn't focus at all but flowed away instead like beer on a table top. "I don't like this dark beyond the window. I don't like it at all."

But the six slugs of Kubanskaya were already approaching my heart, quietly . . . one by one they were approaching my heart, and my heart entered into single combat with reason.

"So what don't you like about the dark? Dark is dark,

and you can't do anything about it. Dark is followed by light and light is followed by dark—that's my opinion. And if you don't like it, the dark won't cease to be dark just because of that. So there remains only one way out: accept the dark. It's not for us fools to get the better of nature's laws. Having stopped up our left nostril we can blow our nose only with the right one. Isn't that so? Well, then, there's no demanding light beyond the window if beyond the window it is dark.

"Yeah that's true . . . but, you know, I did leave in the morning. At eight-sixteen, from the Kursk Station."

"So what if it was morning? Now, thank God, it's autumn, the days are short—you aren't even able to come to and, bang, it's dark again. And you know, it's oh-h-h so long to Petushki. From Moscow to Petushki is oh-h-h so long."

"What sort of oh-h-h? Why're you all the time oh-h-hing? From Moscow to Petushki is exactly two hours and fifteen minutes. Last Friday, for example . . ."

"What's last Friday got to do with it? Who cares about last Friday! Last Friday the train hardly made any stops. And, in general, trains traveled faster then, but now, the devil knows, they stop and wait. For what? It's enough to make you sick sometimes. Why is it always stopping? Like that at every marker. Except Esino."

I glanced out the window and frowned again.

"Yes-s-s, it is strange. We left at eight in the morning and we're still going."

Here, my heart really exploded:

"And the others? What about the others? Are they worse than you? The others, they're also riding along and not asking why it's so long and why it's so dark. They ride along quietly looking out the window. Why do you have to ride quicker than they? It's funny to listen to you, Venya, funny and disgusting. If you've had a drink, Venya, then don't be so immodest, don't think that you're more intelligent and better than others. . . ."

Now this tired me out completely. I went back into the car and sat down on a bench, trying not to look out the window. Everyone in the car, five or six people, were dozing with their heads lowered like babies. I, too, was almost dozing off . . .

And suddenly jumped up from my place. "Gracious Lord! But she's supposed to be waiting for me at eleven in the morning. At eleven she's supposed to be waiting for me and outside it's still dark. So, I'll have to wait for her until morning. I don't really know where she lives. I've been there twelve times, always by way of some back yards and completely smashed. How annoying that on the thirteenth time I'm going to see her I'm completely sober. Because of that I'll have to wait until it finally gets light. Until it finally dawns on my thirteenth Friday.

"But, wait. As I left Moscow, it was already the dawn of my thirteenth Friday. Which means that today is Friday. Why is it so dark outside?"

"Again! Again you're at it with your darkness. Whadaya want with this darkness?"

"But really, last Friday . . ."

"Again, your last Friday. I see, Venya, that you are completely in the past. I see that you don't wish to speak of the future at all."

"No, no, listen . . . Last Friday, exactly at eleven in the

morning, she was there on the platform with her braid from head to tail . . . and it was quite light out; I remember perfectly and I remember her braid perfectly . . ."

"What's her braid got to do with it? I repeat: the days are diminishing because it is autumn. Last Friday at eleven in the morning, I don't argue, it was light. But this Friday at eleven in the morning it may be so dark that you could poke your eye out. Do you know how the days are diminishing now? Do you know? I see that you don't know everything, you only brag about knowing everything. You were also talking to me about the braid! Well, a braid grows—maybe since last Friday it's below her tail. But autumn days, on the other hand, they're little snips . . ."

"All the same, what a dope you are, Venya."

I hit myself not very hard across the cheek, drank three slugs, and shed a tear. From the bottom of my soul, in place of alarm, love arose. I went all limp. "You promised her purple lilies and you're taking her 300 grams of 'Cornflower' candy. And, look, twenty minutes from now you'll be in Petushki and, on the platform bathed in sunlight, you'll get confused and hand her the 'Cornflower.' And everyone around will be saying:

"For the thirteenth time running we've seen nothing but 'Cornflower.' And we've never once seen any lilies or purple. And she'll burst out laughing and say . . ."

Here, I almost dozed off. I dropped my head onto my shoulder and didn't want to raise it again until Petushki. Once more I gave in to the flow . . .

KILOMETER 105—POKROV

But they interfered with my giving in to the flow. No

sooner did I drop off than someone hit me in the back with his tail.

I quivered and turned around. There before me was someone with no feet or tail or head.

"Who are you?" I asked in astonishment.

"Guess who?" And he burst out laughing. With the laugh of a maneater.

"Oh, yeah, you think I'm going to guess?"

I turned away, offended, in order to drop off again. But, here, someone slammed with a crushing blow of his head into my back. I turned around again: there before me was the very same someone without feet or tail or head.

"Why are you hitting me?" I asked him.

"You guess why! . . ." he answered with the same carnivorous laugh.

This time I decided to go ahead and guess. Because if I turned away from this one, for all I knew, he'd crack me in the back with his feet.

I lowered my eyes and fell to thinking. He waited while I thought it out and quietly raised a huge fist right up to my nostrils as if to wipe my snotty nose.

All the same he was the first to speak:

"You're going to Petushki? To the city 'where neither winter nor summer the jasmine never' and so on? Where . . ."

"Right, 'where neither winter nor summer the jasmine never' and so on."

"Where your bucket of slop wallows about in the jasmine and linen and the birds flutter above her and do kiss her wherever they've a mind to?"

"Yes, wherever they've a mind to."

He burst out laughing again and hit me in the pit of my stomach.

"You just listen. Before you, you see a sphinx. And he will not let you into that city."

"Why won't he let me into it? There, in Petushki, what's wrong? The pestilence? Did someone get betrothed to his own daughter there? And you . . ."

"It's worse than a daughter or the pestilence. It's for me to know what's wrong. But I told you I won't let you in, so I won't let you in. Or, I'll let you in on one condition: that you guess the answers to five of my riddles."

"What does he need with his riddles, the viper?" I thought to myself. And said aloud:

"Well, so don't wear me out, let's have your riddles. Take your huge fist away, don't beat me in the pit of my stomach, and let's have your riddles."

"What does he need with his riddles, the fucking huckster?" I thought a second time. But he had already begun his first:

"The well-known shock-worker Aleksei Stakhanov went to the toilet for number one two times a day and once for number two. But when he was on a drunk, he went four times for number one and not once for number two. Calculate how many times per year shock-worker Aleksei Stakhanov went for number one and how many for number two, if we consider that he was on a drunk three hundred and twelve days per year."

I thought to myself: "Who is he hinting about, the brute? Doesn't ever go to the toilet? Who is he hinting about, the slime?"

I got offended and said, "That's a bad riddle, Sphinx, that's a riddle with piggish implications. I won't try to answer a riddle like that."

"Aw, you won't? Well, well. So you're going to start in on me again! Listen to the second:

"When the ships of the American Seventh Fleet docked at the Petushki Station, there were no Communist Party girls present, but if Komsomol girls are considered Party members, then every third one of them was a blonde. When the ships of the American Seventh Fleet set sail, the following was discovered: every third Komsomol girl turned out to have been raped, every fourth rape victim turned out to be a Komsomol girl, every fifth one of the Komsomol girls who had been raped turned out to be a blonde; every ninth blonde rape victim turned out to be a Komsomol member. If there are 428 girls in all in Petushki, determine how many non-Party brunettes among them remained untouched?"

Who, who is he hinting about now, the dog? Why are the brunettes all intact and with the blondes it's nothing but rape? What does he mean to say by this, the parasite?

"I won't try to solve this riddle either, Sphinx. You forgive me, but I won't. It's a very uncouth riddle. Better give me the third."

"Ha, ha! Here's the third:

"As is well known, in Petushki there aren't any points A. Moreover, there are no points B, C, D, or E. There are only points F. So, then, polar explorer Papanin, desiring to save polar explorer Vodopianov, departed from point F_1 for point F_2. At the same moment, Vodopianov, desiring to save Papanin, departed from point F_2 for point F_1. It is not known why both of them turned up at point F_3, located twelve of Vodopianov's spitting distances from point F_1 and sixteen of Papanin's spitting distances from point F_2. If it is allowed that Papanin could spit three meters and seventy-two centimeters and that Vodopianov couldn't spit at all, did Papanin indeed set out to save Vodopianov?"

My God. What's he up to, has he lost his marbles, this mangy sphinx? Where's he headed? Why is it that in Petushki there are no points A, B, C, D, or E, but only F's? What is he hinting at, the bitch?

"Ha, ha," cried the Sphinx, rubbing his hands together. You won't try to solve this one either?! Not this one either?! Got you worried, egghead? Then here's the fourth for you:

"Lord Chamberlain, Premier of the British Empire, while departing the restaurant of the Petushki Railroad Station, slipped on somebody's vomit and, in falling, turned over the next table. On the table, before the fall, there were two pastries at thirty-five kopeks, two portions of beef Stroganoff at seventy-three kopeks each, two portions of udder at thirty-nine kopeks and two carafes each containing 800 grams of sherry. None of the crockery was broken. All the food was ruined. But here's what happened with the sherry: one carafe did not break, but everything spilled out of it to the last drop. The other carafe broke to smithereens, but not a drop spilled out of it. If it is allowed that the cost of an empty carafe is six times more than a portion of udder, while every child knows the cost of sherry, tell me what bill was presented to Lord Chamberlain, Premier of the British Empire, in the Kursk Station restaurant?''

"What do you mean, 'the Kursk Station?' ''

"I mean 'the Kursk Station.' ''

"But didn't he slip—where? He slipped in Petushki. Lord Chamberlain, he slipped in the Petushki restaurant!''

"But he paid the bill at the Kursk Station. How much was the bill?''

Good God! Where do sphinxes like this come from? Without feet, without a head, without a tail, and, what's more, dreaming up such rubbish. And with the snout of a brigand. What's he hinting at, the pig?

"That's no riddle, Sphinx. That's mockery.''

"No, it isn't mockery, Venya. This is a riddle. If you don't like this one, then . . .''

"Then give me the last one, go on.''

"Let's have the last one. Only listen carefully:

"Take our two folk heroes: Minin and, coming toward him, Pozharsky. 'You're acting a bit strange today, Minin,' says Pozharsky, 'like you drank a lot today, 'Yeah, you, too, Pozharsky, you're asleep on your feet.' 'Tell me, sincerely, Minin, how much have you drunk today?' 'I'll tell you right off:

" 'First, 150 grams of Rossiiskaya, then 580 of Kubanskaya, 150 of Stolichnaya, 125 of pepper vodka and 700 grams of beer and vodka mix. And you?' 'I drank exactly the same, Minin.'

" 'So where are you going now, Pozharsky?' 'Where else? To Petushki, of course. And you, Minin?' 'Me too, I'm also going to Petushki. You know, Prince, you're not heading the right way at all!' 'No, it's you who's headed in the wrong direction, Minin.' In other words, they convinced each other that it was necessary to turn back. Pozharsky set off in the direction Minin had been going, and Minin, in Pozharsky's direction. And they both ended up at the Kursk Station.

"So. Now you tell me: if they both had kept the same course and gone their previous directions, where would they have ended up? Where would Pozharsky have gotten to? Tell me."

"To Petushki?" I offered hopefully.

"Not so, as it were. Ha, ha. Pozharsky would have ended up at the Kursk Station. That's where."

And the sphinx burst out laughing and got up on both feet:

"And Minin? Where would Minin have ended up, if he had gone in his own direction and not listened to Pozharsky's advice? Where would Minin have gotten to?"

"Perhaps to Petushki?" I wasn't very hopeful any more and all but started crying. "To Petushki, right?"

"You don't want to try the Kursk Station?! Ha, ha. Minin too will get to the Kursk Station. So which of them will end up at Petushki, ha, ha? Nobody, in general, ha, ha, will end up in Petushki!"

What sort of laugh was it that this scoundrel had? Not once in my life had I heard such blood-curdling laughter. If only he had just laughed—but then, still laughing, he grabbed me by the nose with two of his members and pulled me off somewhere.

"Where, where are you dragging me to, Sphinx? Where are you dragging me to?"

"You'll soon see where. Ha, ha! You'll see."

POKROV—KILOMETER 113

He dragged me out to the vestibule, turned me around with my face to the window and dissolved into thin air. What did he have to do that for?

I looked out the window. Now the old blackness beyond the window was no longer there. On the sweaty glass someone's finger had marked: ". . . ." And through these little gaps I caught sight of city lights, lots of city lights and a station sign swimming past—"Pokrov."

"Pokrov! A town in the Petushki Region. Three stops and then Petushki. You're on the right path, Venedikt Erofeev." And then my alarm, which had risen from the bottom of my soul, started back toward the bottom of my soul and fell quiet there. But then something else started up again from the bottom of my soul—one thought, one monstrous thought rushed upon me so that I felt weak in the knees.

Here I am leaving the Pokrov Station. I saw the sign "Pokrov" and the bright lights. All this bodes well, both "Pokrov" and the bright lights. But why did they appear on the right side of the train? I admit that my reason is in a bit of an eclipse, but, really, I'm no kid, I do know that if the Pokrov Station appears on the right it means I'm going away from Petushki toward Moscow and not away from Moscow toward Petushki. Oh, that mangy sphinx! I was struck dumb and started to rush about the car; as luck would have it there wasn't a soul in it. "Hold it, Venichka, don't rush it. Stupid heart, don't beat. Maybe you've gotten a little confused, maybe Pokrov was on the left and not the right after all? Go on out and take a better look at what side of the train the glass was marked on."

I leapt to the end of the car and looked on the right: on the sweaty glass clearly and prettily was written ". . . ." I looked on the left: there too was written ". . . ." I grabbed my head and returned to the car and again was struck dumb and started to rush about.

"Hold it . . . do you remember, Venichka, the whole way from Moscow you sat on the left side of the train, and all the black moustaches and Mitriches and Decembrists sat on the right? Which means that if you're going in the right direction, your suitcase should be lying on the left side of the train. See, it's so simple!"

I ran the length of the car looking for my suitcase. My suitcase was nowhere to be found—not on the right, not on the left.

Where is my suitcase?!

"Well, OK, OK, Venya, calm down. So what? The suitcase is nonsense, you'll find the suitcase later. First, make up your mind—where you're going. Then look for your suitcase later. First, get it clear in your mind, then later the suitcase. Make up your mind or the million in cash, which? Of course, first the mind, then the million."

"You've got class, Venya. Drink the rest of the Kubanskaya to the fact that you've got class."

And so I threw back my head and drank up my last drop. And right away the dark into which I had been plunged cleared away, and dawn broke in the very depths of my soul and my reason, and sheet lightning glimmered once for every swallow.

"Man should not be lonely—that's my opinion. Man should give of himself to people, even if they don't want to take. But if he is lonely anyway, he should go through the cars. He should find people and tell them: 'Look. I'm lonely. I'll give of myself to the last drop (because I just drank up the last drop, ha-ha!) and you give of yourselves to me and, having given, tell me where are we going. From Moscow to Petushki or from Petushki to Moscow?'"

"And according to you, man should act just like that?" I asked myself, inclining my head to the left.

"Yes. Just like that," I answered myself, inclining my head to the right. "It's not the place for examining '. . . .' on sweaty glass and agonizing over riddles."

And I set off through the train. No one was in the first car; rain splashed in through the open windows. In the second there wasn't anybody either; the rain wasn't even splashing in.

In the third, there was someone. . . .

KILOMETER 113—OMUTISHCHE

. . . A woman, all in black from head to foot, was standing by a window and distractedly looking at the gloom outside; she pressed a lace handkerchief to her lips. "Like two peas in a pod: a copy of *Inconsolable Grief*, a copy of you, Erofeev," I thought, and at once burst out laughing to myself.

Quickly, on tiptoe, so as not to scare off the enchantment, I crept up to her from behind. The woman was crying.

See! Man goes off by himself to have a cry. But, primevally, he is not lonely. When man cries he simply does not want anyone to be party to his tears. And he's justified, for is there anything on earth higher than that which is inconsolable?

"Princess," I called quietly.

"So whadaya want?" the Princess responded, gazing out the window.

"Nothing . . ."

"Then you'd better sit down and shut up—you'll look positively intelligent."

Is it for me—in my position—to be silent? Me, who went through all the cars for the solution to the riddle? Pity that I forgot what the riddle was about. But I remember it was something very important. OK, later I'll think of it. A woman is crying and that is much more important. Oh, shameful beings! You have transformed my earth into the shittiest hell, and you force us to hide tears from people and to put laughter up for show. Oh, miserable scum. You have left people with nothing except "sorrow" and "fear" and, after that, their laughter is public but their tears are banned.

Oh, to say it now, so as *to burn them*, the beasts, *with my fiery word*.

"Princess, oh, Princess . . ."

"So whadaya want again?"

"Hey, listen, Princess. Where is your valet, Peter? I haven't seen him since August."

"What're you spouting?"

144

"Honestly, I haven't seen him since . . . Where's he, your valet?"

"Same place as yours," the Princess snapped. And suddenly she tore away from her place and strode toward the doors, sweeping the floor of the car with her dress. Right at the doors she stopped, turned her husky, cracked, tear-stained face toward me and cried, "I hate you, Tsar Andrei Mikhailovich! I ha-te you." And disappeared.

"So that's i-i-it," I drawled triumphantly, as the Decembrist had, recently. "She really told me off." And left just like that, not answering about important things. Mother of Heaven, what was that important thing? In the name of your gifts, let me recall! "Valet!"

I rang the bell. . . . An hour later I rang again.

"Va-a-let!!"

A servant came in dressed completely in yellow, my valet by the name of Peter. When I was drunk once I had somehow convinced him to wear all yellow till his dying day, the fool, and he'd dressed in it since then. "You know what, Peter? Was I asleep just now, or not? What do you think? Was I asleep?"

"In the other car, yes."

"But in this one, no?"

"No, not in this one."

"That amazes me, Peter. . . . Light the candelabra. Otherwise, you know, I'll become alarmed again. . . . So, Peter, if I'm to believe you, I was asleep in the other car, but awoke in this one. Right?"

"I don't know. I was asleep myself in this car."

"Hm. Good. But why didn't you get up and wake me? Why?"

"And why should I get up and wake you? There was no reason for waking you in this car, when you woke up in here by yourself."

"Don't get me mixed up, Peter, don't mix me up. Let's remember. You see, Peter, I wasn't able to resolve one single thought. And how great this thought is."

"What thought is that?"

"This: do I have anything left to drink?

OMUTISCHE—LEONOVO

"No, no. Don't think that that is really the thought; that is simply the means by which to resolve it. You understand, when the booze leaves the heart, fears and shakiness of consciousness appear. If I'd drink something now, I wouldn't be so broken-up and incoherent. . . . It isn't very noticeable, is it, that I'm broken up?"

"Nothing at all is noticeable. Only your fat face is swollen."

"Oh, that's nothing. The face is nothing. . . ."

"And there's also nothing to drink," Peter offered, and he got up and lit the candelabra.

I shook myself: "It's a good thing you lit them, good, otherwise, know what? It's a bit alarming. We keep going on the whole night and there's no one with us, except us.

"But where's your Princess, Peter?"

"She got off long ago."

"Where did she get off?"

"At Khrapunovo. She was riding from Petushki to Khrapunovo. She got on at Orekhovo-Zuevo and got off at Khrapunovo."

"What Khrapunovo is that? What do you keep spouting, Peter? Don't you mix me up, don't mix me up . . . So, so . . . the most important thought . . . I've got Anton Chekhov on my mind for some reason. Yes, and Friedrich Schiller, Friedrich Schiller and Anton Chekhov. And why, I haven't the vaguest. Right, right . . . now it's getting clearer: Friedrich Schiller, when he sat down to write a tragedy, he'd stick his feet into champagne. Actually, no, that wasn't Schiller. That was State Counselor Goethe, he'd walk around the house in slippers and a bathrobe. But I, no—I go around the house without a bathrobe, I go on the street in slippers. And what's Schiller got to do with it anyway? Yes, here's what: when it happened that he drank vodka, he'd put his feet into champagne, soak and drink. Good. But Chekhov, before he died, he said, 'I want a drink.' And died. . . ."

Peter kept looking at me, standing above me, watching as I collected my thoughts. There was also Hegel. That I remember well: there was Hegel. He'd say, "There are no distinctions, except distinctions in degree, between various degrees and the absence of distinction." That is, if you translate it into good language: "Who doesn't drink these days?"

"Do we have anything to drink, Peter?"

"No, nothing. It's all gone."

"And there isn't anyone on the whole train?"

"No."

"So . . ."

I fell to thinking again. And strange was my thought. It was enveloped around something in such a way that it itself was enveloped in something. And that "something" was also strange. And my soul, my soul was heavy.

What was I doing just then, falling asleep or waking up?

I don't know, and how could I know? "There's a state, but there's no name for it, not sleep nor waking is it." I dozed like that for about twelve or thirty-five minutes.

And when I came to there wasn't a soul in the car, and Peter had disappeared somewhere. The train continued to race through the rain and the blackness. It was strange to listen to the slamming of doors in all the cars, strange because there wasn't a single soul in any of the cars.

I lay there like a corpse, in icy perspiration, and fear kept building under my heart.

"Va-a-let."

Peter appeared in the door with a bluish, evil face. "Come over here, Peter, come over here. You're also all wet, why? That was you just now slamming the doors, right?"

"I wasn't slamming anything. I was asleep."

"Who was slamming the doors then?"

Peter looked at me without blinking.

"Oh, that's nothing, nothing. If alarm is growing under your heart, you've got to stifle it, and in order to stifle it, you've got to have a drink. But do we have anything to drink?"

"No, nothing. It's all gone."

"And isn't there anyone at all in the whole world?"

"No one."

"You're lying, Peter, you're always lying to me! If there isn't anyone else, then who's banging around with the doors and windows? Huh? Do you know? Do you hear? You've got something to drink, no doubt, and you keep lying to me!"

Peter was looking at me, always the same, unblinking

and spiteful. I saw by his ugly face that I had gotten to the core of him, that I understood him, and that now he feared me. Yes, yes, he had fiddled around with the candelabrum and put it out himself, and then went along through the car putting out the lights. "He's ashamed, ashamed," I thought. But he had already jumped out the window.

I cried, "Come back, Peter," in a voice even I couldn't recognize. "Come back!"

"Trickster!" he answered from behind the window.

And suddenly he flitted back into the car again and flew up to me, and tore at my hair with the most desperate spite.

"What's with you, Peter? What's with you?!"

"Nothing. Stay, stay on here, hag. Stay, old bitch! Go on to Moscow. Sell your seeds there. I can't stand it, I can't st-a-a-and it."

And once more he flitted away, this time for good.

"The devil knows what's up. What's with the bunch of them?" I squeezed my temples, shuddered and shook. The train shuddered and shook with me.

LEONOVO—PETUSHKI

The doors started to click, then to bang louder and louder, more and more clearly. And then into my car and through it flew the tractor driver Evtushenkin, his face blue with fear. And a dozen moments later, the very same way, a horde of Erinyes raced after him, tambourines and cymbals clanging.

My hair stood on end. Forgetting myself, I stamped my feet: "Stop, girls! Goddesses of vengeance, stop! No one

149

in the world is guilty." But they all ran on, and when the last one drew even with me, I was boiling and grabbed her from behind. She was panting.

"Where are you going? Where are you all running to?"

"Whadaya want? Unhand me, let go!"

"Where? Where are we all going??"

"And what business is it of yours, cr-a-a-a-zy man? . . ."

And suddenly she turned toward me, clasped my head and kissed me on the forehead so unexpectedly that I became embarrassed, sat down and started to nibble on a sunflower seed.

And as I was nibbling away, she returned and slammed past my left cheek. She slammed past it, soared toward the ceiling, and rushed off after the others. I tore after her.

The sun was ablaze in the west and the horses shied, and where is that happiness which they write about in the newspapers? I ran and ran through whirlwind and gloom, ripping doors off their hinges. I realized that the Moscow—Petushki train was flying off over the embankment. The cars heaved upward, then fell back again, as if overcome by stupor. And then I started to rush about crying:

"O-o-o-oh! St-o-o-o-p! A-a-ah!"

And was struck dumb. The chorus of Erinyes was racing back from the head of the train straight at me in a panic-stricken herd. Evtushenkin, white with rage, was chasing after them. The whole mass knocked me down and buried me underneath their feet.

They went on clanging their cymbals and clattering their

tambourines. And stars fell on the porch of the Agro-Soviet. And the maid of Shulam roared with laughter.

And then everything started to swirl around. If you say that it was fog, I probably would agree with you—yes, it was fog. But if you say, "No, it wasn't fog, it was fire and ice," probably you're right—fire and ice. That is, at first the blood grows cold, grows cold—and the moment it freezes, it starts boiling and, having boiled up, it grows cold again.

"I've got a fever," I thought, "this hot fog everywhere, it's from a fever because I'm shivering myself and there's hot fog everywhere. And someone very familiar appears from out of the fog, Achilles—not Achilles but very familiar. Oh, now I see, it's the Pontic King Mithridates, all smeared with snot, with a penknife in his hand . . .

"Mithridates, that you, is it?" I said, barely able to make sounds. "That you, is it, Mithridates?"

"It is I," the Pontic King answered.

"And why are you all smeared up?"

"I'm always like this—come the full moon and the snot starts running."

"It doesn't at other times?"

"Sometimes it does, but not like during the full moon."

"And what about it, don't you wipe your nose at all?" I asked, almost whispering. "Don't you?"

"Oh, what can I say? Sometimes I do, but in the full of the moon can you actually wipe it? Not so much as you smear it around. Really, everybody's got his own style. Some will let it run, others will wipe it, still others will smear it around. But me, in the full of the moon . . ."

I interrupted him:

"You talk a good game, Mithridates, but what do you have the knife in your hand for?"

"What do you think? He's asking! To cut you up with, that's what for!"

And how he changed suddenly. He had talked quietly all the while, but now he bared his teeth, turned black—and where did all the snot get to? And, on top of that, he roared with laughter again. Then he bared his teeth again, then again roared with laughter.

I was hit by the shivers once more. "What are you up to, Mithridates?" I whispered or cried, I don't know which. "Get rid of the knife, what do you need with a knife?" But he couldn't hear anything anymore. He threatened me; it was as if a thousand devils possessed him.

"Savage!"

And then he stabbed me in the left side, and I started to moan quietly, because I didn't even have the strength to try to raise my arm to protect myself from the knife. "Stop it, Mithridates, stop it . . ."

But he stabbed me in the right side, then the left again, then the right. I only succeeded in screaming helplessly and rushing about the platform in pain. I woke up with cramps all over. There was nothing around except the wind, the dark, and devilish cold. "What's with me and where am I? Why is it drizzling? Oh, God . . ."

And I fell asleep again. And again it started up the same, the shivers and the heat and the fever and, from far off, over there where the fog swirled, those two lanky figures from Mukhina's huge sculpture emerged, the worker with his hammer and the peasant woman with her sickle, and they came right up to me, both with smirks on their faces. And the worker hit me on the head with his hammer and then the peasant woman gave it to me in the balls with her sickle. I cried out, probably aloud, and woke up once more; this time I was in convulsions, everything in me was shuddering—my face and clothes and soul and thoughts.

Oh, this pain. Oh, this devilish cold. Oh, the impossibility of it. If every one of the Fridays ahead is like this one, some Thursday I'll hang myself. I was expecting some other kind of convulsions from you, Petushki. While I was getting to you, who cut up your birds and trampled on your jasmine? Queen of Heaven, I am in Petushki!

"It's nothing, Erofeev, it's nothing . . . *Talife cumi*, as the Savior said; that is, get up and go. I know, I know, you're beat, in all your members and in the depths of your soul, and it's wet and empty here on the platform and nobody met you and no one will ever meet you. All the same, get up and go. Try it . . . But, God, your suitcase with the goodies? Two cups of nuts for the kid, 'Cornflower' candy and the empty bottle . . . Where's your suitcase? Who stole it? After all, it had the goodies in it. But take a look, do you have any money, maybe just a little? Yes, yes, a little, hardly anything. But what good is money now? Oh, the ephemeral. Oh, vanity. Oh, that most infamous and shameful of times in the life of my people—the time from the closing of the liquor stores until dawn!

"It's nothing, Erofeev, nothing. *Talife cumi*, as your

Tsaritsa said when you were lying in your coffin; that is, arise, brush off your coat, clean up your pants, shake the dust off, and go on. Try two steps, anyway, the rest will be easier. You yourself told your little boy when he was sick, 'One-two-button-your-shoe, aren't-you-ashamed-to-be-lying-in-bed . . .' The main thing is to get off the tracks; trains are always going by here, from Moscow to Petushki, from Petushki to Moscow. Get off the tracks. Then you'll find out why there's not a soul around and why she didn't meet you and everything. Go on, Venichka, go on.''

PETUSHKI. STATION SQUARE

"If you want to go to the left, Venichka, go to the left. If you want to go right, go right. It's all the same, so you might as well follow your nose . . .''

Someone told me once that it's very simple to die: to do it you've got to breathe in forty times altogether, deep, deep, as deep as you can, and breathe out the same way, from the depths of your heart, and then you'll let go of your soul. Maybe I should try it?

Oh, hold it! Maybe I should find out what time it is. But who can I ask, if there's not a single soul in the square, not a single one? And if some living soul did come along, could you even get your mouth open with the cold and the grief? Yes. Oh, the muteness of the cold and the grief!

And if I die sometime—I'm going to die very soon—I know I'll die as I am, without accepting this world, perceiving it close up and far away, inside and out, perceiving but not accepting it. I'll die and He will ask me: "Was it good there for you? Was it bad there for you?" I will be silent, with lowered eyes. I'll be silent with that muteness familiar to everyone who knows the outcome of days of hard boozing. For isn't the life of man a momentary booziness of the soul? And an eclipse of the soul as well? We are all as if drunk, only everybody in his own way: one person has drunk more, the next less. And it works differently on each: the one laughs in the face of this world, while the next cries on its bosom. One has already thrown up and feels better, while the next is only starting to feel like throwing up. But me, what am I? I've partaken of much, but nothing works on me. I haven't really laughed properly, even once, and I've never thrown up, even once. I, who have partaken of so much in this world that I've lost count and the sequence of it all, I am soberer than anyone else in this world; it's simply that nothing much works on me. "Why are you silent?" the Lord, all in blue lightning, asks me. So, what shall I answer him? I'll just be silent, silent . . .

Maybe I should open my mouth after all? Find some living soul and ask for the time?

What do you need the time for, Venichka? Better go on, back to the wind, and get going bit by bit. Once you had a heavenly paradise, you could have found out the time last Friday, but now your heavenly paradise is no more, what do you need with the time? Your Tsaritsa did not come to you on the platform with her lashes lowered. A deity has turned away from you, so what do you need to find out the time for? "Not a woman but blancmange," as you once called her in jest, she didn't come to you on the platform. The delight of humankind, the lily of the valley, did not come to meet you. What's the point of finding out the time after that, Venichka?

What's left to you? In the morning to moan, in the evening to cry, at night to grind your teeth. And who, who in the world cares about your heart? Who? Just go into any home in Petushki, knock on any door and ask, "What do you care about my heart?" Oh, my God . . .

I went around the corner and knocked on the first door I came to.

PETUSHKI. SADOVY CIRCLE

I knocked and stood shivering in the cold waiting for them to open the door. "Strange, the tall buildings they've put up in Petushki. However, it's always like that with a long, hard drunk: people seem hideously angry, the streets excessively wide, the houses terribly big . . . Everything gets bigger with a hangover, exactly as much as everything seemed more insignificant than usual when you were drunk. Do you remember the premise of that guy with the black moustache?"

I knocked again, a little harder than before.

"Is it really so difficult to open the door to someone and let him in to warm up for three minutes? I don't understand it. They, they're serious and don't understand it, but I'm a lightweight and I'll never understand it . . . *Mene, tekel, parsin,* that is, you are weighed upon the scales and found wanting—that is, *tekel.* So let it be, let it . . .

"But if there are scales or not, all the same, on those scales sighs and tears outweigh calculation and design. I know that better than you know anything. I've lived through a lot, I've drunk and thought through a lot and I know what I'm saying. All your guiding stars are rolling toward the horizon and, if not, they're barely glimmering. I don't know you, people, I know you badly. I rarely paid any attention to you, but I've got something for you: I'm concerned with what your souls are taken with, now, in order to know for sure whether the Star of Bethlehem will blaze forth once again or once again start to glimmer. Because all the others are rolling toward the horizon, or if they aren't, they're barely glimmering—and even if they are, they aren't worth two gobs of spit.

"If there are scales there or not—there, we lightweights will outweigh and overcome. I believe in that more firmly than you believe in anything. I believe, I know, and I bear witness to it to the world. But it's strange how the streets have gotten so wide in Petushki . . ."

I moved away from the door and wearily gazed from one house to the other, from one front hallway to the other. And while a single oppressive thought terrible to pronounce together with an oppressive conjecture also terrible to pronounce clawed at me, I went on and on, and I stared intently at every house, with difficulty. There were tears in my eyes, from the cold and from something else.

"Don't cry, Erofeev, don't cry . . . Why should you? And why are you shaking so? From the cold and from something else, too? You needn't . . ."

If I had had twenty swallows of Kubanskaya, they would have gone to the heart and the heart would have been able to convince reason that I was in Petushki. But I didn't have any Kubanskaya. I turned onto a back street and once again started to shake and to cry. . . .

And here something happened more terrifying than anything seen in a dream. In the very same back street, four men came toward me. I recognized them at once—I won't tell you who they were—I started shaking even more than before, convulsively.

They came up and surrounded me. How can I explain to you what sort of ugly faces they had? No, not at all like brigands—rather, there was a touch of something classical about them. But the eyes of all four—have you ever sat in the toilet in the Petushki Station and do you remember how, far below the round openings, that reddish-brown piss-water splashes and glitters? That's the kind of eyes they all had. And the fourth one looked like . . . I'll tell you later whom the fourth one looked like.

"Well, now you've had it," one of them said.

"What do you mean, 'I've had it'?" My voice was trembling terribly, from the hangover and from the chill. They assumed that it was from fear.

"Like this, you've had it! And you're not going anywhere ever again."

"Why?"

"Because."

"Listen . . ." My voice broke. Now my every nerve was trembling, not only my voice. At night no one can be sure of himself—that is, I mean to say, on a cold night. The Apostle betrayed Christ before the third cock crew. Rather, the Apostle betrayed Christ thrice before the cock crew. I know why he betrayed Him: because he was shivering from the cold. He was still warming himself by the fire, together with *them*. But I don't have a fire, no, and I've been boozing for a week. And if they were to torture me now, I would betray him to the seven times seventieth time and more . . .

"Listen," I said to them, the best I could. "You let me go . . . what am I to you? I just didn't get to my girl . . . I was on my way but didn't get there, I just overslept. They stole my suitcase while I was asleep, it had a little stuff in it, but it's a pity all the same . . . The 'Cornflower' . . ."

"What's a cornflower got to do with it?" one of them asked spitefully.

"Oh, candy, 'Cornflower' candy . . . and 200 grams of nuts, taking them to the kid; I promised him because he really knows his alphabet letter . . . but that's nonsense . . . Once it gets light I'll start out again . . . without money, without presents, but they'll understand, they won't say a thing . . . on the contrary."

All four stared at me intently and all four probably thought, "The bum, what a coward, how transparent!" Oh, let them, let them think it, if only they'd let me go! Where, in what newspaper, have I seen their repulsive faces?

"I want to go to Petushki again . . ."

"You're not going to any Petushki!!"

"Well, suppose I don't, then I want to go to the Kursk Station."

"There won't be any station for you!"

"And why not?"

"Just because!"

One of them swung his arm and hit me in the cheek; another, with his fist, in my face; the two others moved in, too. All the same, I remained standing and moved off quietly, quietly, quietly, but all four kept quietly after me.

"Run, Venichka, any place at all, doesn't matter where. Run to the Kursk Station. To the left or the right or back, it doesn't matter where you end up. Run, Venichka, run . . ."

I grabbed myself by the head and started running. With them behind me.

PETUSHKI. THE KREMLIN.

"Maybe this is Petushki after all? . . . Why aren't there any people on the streets? Have they all died off? If the four of them catch up, they'll kill me . . . and who'll be there to hear my screaming? There's not a single light in any window, but—it's fantastic—the street lights are shining, shining without batting an eye.

"It's very possible this is Petushki. That building straight ahead over there, it's the Regional Social Welfare Agency, there, beyond, it's dark. The Petushki Social Welfare Agency and, beyond, dark forever and ever and the resting place of departed souls. Oh, no, no!"

I leapt out into a square covered with wet paving stones, took a breath and looked around.

"No, this isn't Petushki! If He, if He has departed the earth forever but sees every one of us, I know that He never once looked this way . . . And if He never left the earth, if He has passed through it barefoot and dressed as a slave, He passed this place by and went off somewhere . . .

"No, this isn't Petushki. He did not pass Petushki by. He was tired and took his rest in Petushki and I have noticed in many souls there the ashes and smoke of his campfire . . .

"No, this isn't Petushki!" The Kremlin shone before me

160

in all its splendor. Even though I heard the clattering pursuit behind me, I had time to think: "I, who have passed through all Moscow, up and down, drunk and sober, I've never seen the Kremlin, and, when I went hunting for it, I always ended up at the Kursk Station. And now, finally, I see it when the Kurst Station is more necessary to me than anything on earth!

"Inscrutable are your ways . . ."

They were getting closer and closer, and I couldn't seem to catch my breath in order to run on. I could only drag myself over to the Kremlin wall and collapse.

They came across the Square, two from either side. "Who are they and what have I done to them?" It didn't occur to me to ask. "Who cares? Either they'll see me or they won't—who cares, anyway? There's no need to tremble, what I need is rest, that is my desire . . . Deliver me, Lord . . ."

But they spotted me. Came up and surrounded me, puffing heavily. It's a good thing I was able to get up on my feet—they would have killed me.

"You wanted—you wanted to run away from us?" one of them hissed, and grabbed me by the hair, slamming my head into the Kremlin wall with all his strength. It seemed to me that I split in two from the pain. Blood streamed down my face and under my collar. I almost fell but managed to remain standing. They started to beat me up.

"Give it to him in the guts, with your boot in the guts. Let him squirm!"

My God! I broke away and ran off down the Square. "Run, Venichka, if you can, run off, they can't run at all." I stopped for two moments by the monument and wiped the blood from my eyes in order to see better. I first looked at Minin and then at Pozharsky, then Minin again—where, which direction should I run? Where is the Kursk Station and where should I run? There was no time to think; I ran off in the direction in which Prince Dmitri Pozharsky was looking.

MOSCOW/PETUSHKI. AN UNIDENTIFIED FRONT HALLWAY

Right up to the very last moment, I was still counting on saving myself. Even when I ran into some strange front hallway, climbed up to the top landing and collapsed again, I still kept on hoping. "Oh, it's nothing, nothing, your heart will quiet down in an hour, you'll wash off the blood, lie down, Venichka, lie down till morning and then you'll go to the Kursk Station and . . . You don't need to shake like that, I already told you, you don't have to . . ."

My heart was beating so it was difficult to hear and all the same I heard—the door below opened slowly and, for five moments, didn't close again.

Trembling all over, I said to myself, *Talife cumi,* that is, "Get up and prepare for the end . . ." This isn't *Talife cumi,* it's *lama savahfani,* as the Savior said . . . That is, "Why hast thou forsaken me?"

The Lord was silent.

Angels of heaven, they're coming up, what should I do? What should I do, now, so as not to die? Angels!

And the angels burst out laughing. Do you know how angels laugh? They are shameful creatures . . . should I tell you how they burst out laughing just now? A long time ago, in Lobna—at the station—a man was cut up by a train, cut up in an unbelievable way: his whole lower half was crushed to smithereens and scattered over the road bed, but his upper half from the belt up remained as if alive, and stood by the tracks, the way busts of various pigs stand on pedestals. The train pulled away but he— that half of him—remained standing there, and on his face there was a sort of perplexity and his mouth half open. A lot of people couldn't stand to look at it and turned away, pale, with a deathly weariness in their hearts. But some children ran up to him, three or four children, they had picked up a lighted cigarette butt from somewhere and stuck it in the dead man's half-open mouth. And the cigarette butt continued to smoke and the children ran around roaring with laughter.

That's how the heavenly angels laughed at me then. They laughed, and God was silent . . . And I had already caught sight of the four of them, they were climbing up from the floor just below. But when I saw them, I was really more surprised than afraid. All four of them were climbing the stairs barefoot, with their shoes in their hands. Why was this necessary? So as not to make noise in the hall? Or in order to sneak up on me unnoticed? I don't know, but it was the last thing that I remember. That is, this feeling of surprise.

They didn't even stop to rest, but rushed from the top of the stair to strangle me, right away, five or six hands. I tried to untangle their hands and defend my throat as best I could. And then the worst thing of all happened: the one with the fiercest and most classical profile pulled a huge awl with a wooden handle out of his pocket, maybe not even an awl but a screwdriver or something else, I don't know. But he ordered all the others to hold my hands, and no matter how I tried to defend myself they pinned me down to the floor, half-crazy.

"What for? What-for-what-for-what-for?" I muttered.

They stuck their awl into my throat.

I didn't know that there was pain like that in the world. And I writhed from the torture of it—a clotted red letter "*Ю*" spread across my eyes and started to quiver. And since then I have not regained consciousness, and I never will.

While working as
a cable fitter in
Sheremetievo,
Autumn, 1969.